THE SECRET STORY OF
Sonia Rodriguez

by Alan Lawrence Sitomer

Disney • JUMP AT THE SUN

Los Angeles   New York

Also by Alan Lawrence Sitomer

The Hoopster

The Hoopster: A Teacher's Guide

Hip-Hop Poetry and the Classics

Hip-Hop High School

Homeboyz

Nerd Girls: The Rise of the Dorkasauraus

Nerd Girls: A Catastrophe of Nerdish Proportions

Caged Warrior

Noble Warrior

Copyright © 2008 by Alan Lawrence Sitomer

All rights reserved. Published by Disney • Jump at the Sun,
an imprint of Disney Book Group. No part of this book may be
reproduced or transmitted in any form or by any means, electronic
or mechanical, including photocopying, recording, or by any
information storage and retrieval system, without written permission
from the publisher. For information address Disney • Jump at the Sun
125 West End Avenue, New York, New York 10023.

Printed in the United States of America

First Hardcover Edition, September 2008
First Paperback Edition, February 2010
10 9 8 7 6 5
FAC-025438-15273

Library of Congress Cataloging-in-Publication Control Number: 2007045265
ISBN 978-1-4231-3027-7

Visit www.hyperionteens.com

SUSTAINABLE
FORESTRY
INITIATIVE
Certified Chain of Custody
Promoting Sustainable Forestry
www.sfiprogram.org
SFI-01054
The SFI label applies to the text stock

For Tracey . . .

chapter uno

I was born in the United States of America. That makes me legal.

Pero mis padres jumped the border to get here. That makes them illegal.

I have documents.

They don't.

I speak English.

They don't.

I have a social security number, a passport, and a license to drive.

They don't. They don't. They don't.

Actually, *mi papi* does have a social security number. Three of them. You can buy them for fifteen dollars apiece down at the *taquería*.

I know it's wrong, but it's not like he's doing anything different from anyone else. One *vato* down the block has fourteen different sets of official state identification cards, like he's the Mexican James Bond or something. That would be funny, James Bond-*zales*, Agent Double O *Siete*.

Maybe I shouldn't write about that. After all, I don't want to get *mi papi* in trouble. He only came here for opportunity.

In Mexico, opportunity doesn't exist. There's too much poverty. If a person isn't born rich, it's almost impossible for them to make a living and support their family—so *mi papi* jumped the border. He hired coyotes, fought off *bandidos*, bribed *policías*, and nearly lost his right hand from poison when he was bit by a yellow scorpion in the middle of the desert.

All that to provide a better life for his children. All that for me.

Now, I know I don't write so good. But I'm a Latina. A first-generation Latina—or "Hispanic American" or "Chicano immigrant" or "wetback *puta*," whatever you want to call me. And people should hear the truth. The real truth.

About my secrets. (Secrets that no one has ever heard before.)

I apologize in advance if my book stinks. Like I said, I know I don't write so good. Yet still, I think my story is important. And some parts are juicy. There is sex and violence and drugs. I know people who read books like that kind of stuff. But there is love too. In my opinion, love stories are the best of all.

But most important, there is truth. And sometimes *la verdad*—the truth—can save your life.

chapter dos

Being the oldest daughter in a *familia* of seven has its benefits. I cook, I clean, I mop, I sweep, I shine, I bake, I dust, I do laundry, change diapers, wipe countertops, and scrub the goopy grime off the tile floor in the shower. I even do windows. Like I said, being the oldest daughter has its benefits:

For everybody else. It's part of *mi cultura*.

Don't get me wrong, I love *mi cultura*. I love it deep in my bones. I love the cooking and the food. I love the music and the dancing. But most of all, I love the people. Smiles, honor, family, *amor*—Latinos have warmth in their blood. I think it's all this warmth that makes our skin turn brown. It's as if the heat of our passion has boiled the liquid in our veins and cooked our flesh from the inside out to make our coloring go crispy brown like a flour tortilla being used to make a delicious quesadilla. Mmmm, I love quesadillas. Especially when they are crispy brown.

Sí, adoro mi cultura.

But I hate my culture, too. I hate that so many stereotypes are true. We do shove fourteen people into a van and drive twenty miles slower than the speed limit in the fast lane of the highway. And we do make lots of *bebés* at a young age and let them run around with bare feet and dirty clothes in front of the *super-mercado*, sucking on candy lollipops. And we do come to this country and speak no English and then act as if there is no reason for us to even learn the language in the first place. *Sí, yo hablo español,* but I speak English too. That's why I am going to write my story in English (well, mostly English), to prove the stereotypes wrong.

If I can.

After all, some stereotypes are too powerful to change. Like the ones about my people and tequila. It's true, we do have a lot of *alcohólicos* in our culture.

Like my *drunkle,* my drunk uncle. He's a mess.

"¡Sonia . . . ayúdame!" mi ama called out. The literal translation of the word *"Ayúdame"* means "Help me," but when my mother calls out *"Ayúdame,"* she rarely means "Help me." She more means, "Do this for me."

And what she was asking me to do was clean up my drunkle. He'd pissed his pants.

It's not uncommon for *alcohólicos* to pass out and pee themselves. You'd think they'd be embarrassed about it, as if the shame of wetting yourself like a two-year-old would be enough to get them to give up the booze bottles. But there's nothing strong enough to get my drunkle to give up the booze bottles. He'd choose tequila over work, family, money, self-respect, and love. Already has, as a matter of fact. He's never held a job, all the *mujeres* in his life have left him due to his rotten ways, and he's taken unfair advantage of his *familia* over and over and over again. So many times that we've all lost count.

But just because he takes advantage of us doesn't mean we turn our backs on him. After all, he's *familia*, and in *mi cultura*, *familia* means more than anything. *Familia es lo primero*, no matter what.

Me, I just wish he'd leave. Disappear. Take off. Or maybe trip and fall and break his back and snap his spine and twist his neck so that he'd be forced to live in a rusty wheelchair for the rest of his life, which we could roll off to another part of the city. I know that sounds really mean, but my drunkle's really mean. I once saw him flick the head of a crying baby to get it to shut up. Of course, this only made the baby cry more.

I was gonna snitch to the baby's mother, too. I really was. After all, I did see it happen, and the poor woman was so freaked out by the mysterious purple-and-black lump on her baby's forehead that she rushed her child to the emergency room and asked the doctors to scan her kid's head for brain tumors.

But I didn't. I couldn't. You just can't. Not when it's *familia*. *Familia* always sticks together, even when we're wrong.

I wish someone would flick him in his head, though. With a baseball bat.

"*Mija*," *mi papi* had said to me when he'd heard how I felt about his brother-in-law, "always remember, do not stoop to that level."

That's what my father always says when I get angry and want to do things I'll later regret. He says, "Do not stoop to that level." I try to listen, but it's hard.

"*Sonia . . .*" *mi ama* called again.

I put down the jar of grape jelly I was using to make a sandwich for one of my younger brothers (who hates peanut butter but loves peanuts, go figure) and went to take off my drunkle's shoes. Since I wasn't stooping to the level of not helping a family member in need, I had to stoop to the level of where my drunkle was lying passed out on the floor in a puddle of his own pee. I reached for his feet while *mi ama* unbuttoned his shirt. Then, after I had my drunkle's socks off, my mother told me to wait in the kitchen so she could unzip his pants, strip his clothes, and wrap him in a towel. Being pregnant with twins made the task of undressing my uncle *muy difícil* for *mi ama*, but still, she didn't want me to help beyond taking off the stuff on his feet. After all, no little girl should ever risk seeing their drunkle's pecker.

His socks were wet and cheesy. I walked back to the kitchen to put on my orange dish gloves because I didn't want any part of my drunkle's clothing to touch my bare skin. In *mi casa* I was like the Spanish Cinderella, except there was no ball, no pumpkin, no fairy godmother, no magic pair of slippers, and there was certainly no Prince Charming anywhere in sight. All I had was a drunkle, a drunk uncle who peed his pants.

Mi ama brought me the dirty clothes. I tried to avoid breathing through my nose but still couldn't avoid inhaling a nasty whiff of urine. Phew! I turned my head and made sure to handle my drunkle's wet underwear as carefully as I could.

Then I dropped them. Right on top of my left foot. Wet piss juice ran between the creases in my toes. Ugh! Stupid me was only wearing flip-flops.

I took a deep breath and tried not to freak out. There were still two more lunches to make for *mis otros hermanos*, a sink full of breakfast dishes to wash, and the laundry to take off the clothesline in the backyard because the weather forecast guy said it might rain. And now I'd have to shower again before class. First day of tenth grade and already I'd be late.

"Sonia . . ." *mi ama* yelled again from the other room. I paused without answering. Maybe if I didn't respond, she'd stop calling for me.

"Sonia . . ." she repeated. "*Ayúdame.*"

Ay, Ama, I thought to myself. I have to get to school.

A moment later I heard a gag. Then my drunkle puked. It was a liquidy vomit, the kind that looked like broth soup with small chunks of light brown meat in it.

"Sonia . . ." *mi ama* called again.

Yep, first day and I'd be really late.

chapter tres

America prides itself on being a melting pot. Only problem is, white people seem to melt a lot less than the rest of the pot. Especially at the bottom of the pot, where us minorities live. One look at my high school tells the whole story. It's *una zona sin gringos*, a Caucasian-free zone.

Sure, we got lots of white teachers, but *no hay estudiantes gringos*. Just blacks and browns, with a few scattered Asians.

I'm not racist, though. In fact, my best friend is black. Her name is Theresa Anderson, but most people just call her "Tee-Ay." And Tee-Ay's way smarter than I am. She already knows lots of words for the SAT, and some of them are over ten letters long. Me, I struggle with high school but I promised myself a long time ago that no matter what, I was going to be the first Rodriguez in America to graduate. For some people that may not sound like much, but for me it's a big deal. A very big deal. Especially because I'm a girl. Of course, no one expects me to do it, but in my heart I am determined, more determined than anyone gives me credit for.

Besides, graduating is the only way I'll ever be able to pay back *mi papi* for all he's done for me. *Mi papi*, he's the best.

I know people think my father is just another illegal, border-jumping, wetback immigrant, but the truth is, everything good I have in this world comes from the sacrifices he's made for me. *Por ejemplo*, my braces just came off last week, and everyone keeps telling me that my teeth look good. The only reason I could even afford to have braces is because *Papi* took a third job selling mini palm trees at a Swap Meet. For three and a half years he woke up every Sunday morning at 4:15 a.m. just so he could buy me a nice smile. When you already have two hard jobs and you take hard job number three, well . . . sometimes when I think about the sacrifices my father has made, I want to cry. There's nothing I wouldn't do for him.

Even geometry. Now that's love.

During lunchtime at my school, some girls do their makeup. Some girls gossip. Some girls sneak off and do things with guys. Dirty, nasty things. Me, I do math homework. Usually I do it while eating french fries and drinking Diet Pepsi with Tee-Ay. In a way, it's our own little *tradición*.

I opened my math book and stared at the problem in front of me. Math hurt my brain. Sometimes it even felt like the equations were staring back at me, like they had beady little eyeballs all their own.

Question #1
JX = XN
4XN + 2 = 14
Find the Value of JN

Question #2
LT = TX
5LT − 3 = 7
Find the Value of XL

NOTE: Figures not drawn to scale

I popped a fry in my mouth and squinched my eyes real hard, trying to concentrate. Geometry was hard, but I needed it to get a diploma.

"Hey, Sonia, what do you think Jimmy Gomez looks like naked?" Tee-Ay asked, not caring that she was interrupting me.

I didn't look up. Maybe she'd drop it if I ignored her. Tee-Ay was always yapping about all kinds of kooky things. I squinched my eyes tighter and felt my forehead crumple. Math was going to give me wrinkles. To find the value of XL I'd need to . . .

"I bet he has pimples on his butt," Tee-Ay continued. "Those big, red juicy kind that when you squeeze 'em, white-and-green pus oozes out."

"¡Jesucristo, Tee!" I said, cutting her off before she got too gross. "Can't you see I have homework?"

Tee-Ay just laughed and ate another french fry. I tried to act as if I wasn't interested in Jimmy Gomez or pimply butts or naked boys, but Tee-Ay knew me too well for me to hide the truth. No, I wasn't interested in Jimmy Gomez. And no, I definitely wasn't interested in pimply butts. But naked boys? Well, I had to admit, the thought of swinging ding-a-lings did make me curious. However, boys puzzle me.

Por ejemplo, I once read that most teenage boys masturbate. And a lot. It said that some of them do it like five or six times a day. I wonder, did it feel that good? Well, it certainly explained why so many of them didn't do their math homework. They're too busy playing with their penises.

Boys are liars, though. I learned that the minute I started to grow boobs. It happened when I was twelve, and a fourteen-year-old Latin-lover type named Enrique started telling me how pretty I was and began asking me out on dates. He had green eyes and dark, caramel skin. But of course, when you're twelve years old you certainly can't go out on dates.

Especially with seventeen-year-olds. That's how old Enrique really was. It turned out that a group of *hombres* had formed a crew called the *coño huntaz* and were having a competition to see which guy could pop the most virgin cherries in our neighborhood. That's why I hate boys. They'll tell you any lie they can about love just to get into your pants.

¡Qué monstruos!

Actually, it was Tee-Ay who found out about the crew and warned me about Enrique. She and I pretty much told each other everything. She's told me about how she couldn't stand being compared to her older brother and how she got caught smoking pot and was almost sent to live in one of those detention camps, and I told her about how my older brother was a total loser and how I once caught my drunkle staring at me in my pajamas like some sort of freaky perv. Right after those words left my mouth about my drunkle, though, I'd wished I'd never said them. Some things about *familia* aren't meant to be told to anybody. Not even to your closest friends.

At least, that's what I used to think. After what happened, though, I learned different.

Anyway, I took a final sip of Diet Pepsi, wiped my hands with a napkin, and turned back to my homework. Lunch was officially over. The thought of a sweaty boy with big, bubbly pimples on his butt had ruined my appetite.

Thanks, Tee.

I squinched my eyes again, relooked at the math problem, and started to do some substitutions.

Question #1
JX = XN
4XN + 2 = 14
Find the Value of JN

Question #2
LT = TX
5LT – 3 = 7
Find the Value of XL

NOTE: Figures not drawn to scale

Question #1	Question #2
JX = XN	LT = TX
4XN + 2 = 14	5LT – 3 = 7
4XN + 2 – 2 = 14 - 2	5LT – 3 + 3 = 7 + 3
4XN = 12	5LT = 10
XN = 3	LT = 2
JX = XN	LT = TX
JX + XN = JN	LT + TX = XL
3 + 3 = JN	2 + 2 = XL
JN = 6	XL = 4

It took me six tries to get it right, but finally I finished. I always finished. I had figured out that completing all of your homework assignments is the secret key to graduating from high school, so last year as a freshman I promised myself that no matter how many classes I had to miss or how often I would be late to school due to *mi familia*, I would always do my homework.

Always.

After all, this was the way of the *tortuguita*. That's the nickname *mi papi* gave me. For years he's called me his little *tortuguita*. I guess for people who know me well, it kinda fits.

chapter cuatro

You know the fairy tale about the *tortuga* and the hare, the one where the crazy rabbit is so fast it can easily win the race but ends up losing in the end to the turtle? That's me, the *tortuguita*. My father says being a *tortuga* is the only way brown people have a chance in this country, and that on the inside I have the great strength of a turtle.

I didn't know if I had any great strength on the inside. And I was less sure if it was even flattering to be nicknamed after a turtle. I mean, come on, at least make me an eagle or a tiger or a mighty falcon or something, but a turtle? However, I did know that when it came to brown people in El Norte, the odds were stacked against us big and tall.

Por ejemplo, my new history teacher had just told us that there were now more brown-skinned men in

American jails than in American universities. *¡Increíble!* Then again, it does seem like everyone I know has at least one relative in prison.

Usually I try to ignore stats like that when I hear them because they hurt too bad. It's just way too depressing to think about the realities of most brown-skinned people here in America: at the health care *clínicas*, the way the *policía* treat us, the fact that we do most of the toilet cleaning in the restrooms of all the hotels, and on and on and on. I mean, there are so many of us here in this country, yet most Latino people live as if we are holding a second-class bus pass on a first-class train. No matter where I go, I feel like an outsider.

I don't complain, though. I'm the type of person who would rather just lock up all my feelings on the inside and drown out the pain, like how La Llorona drowned her children, so I can spare the other parts of me from more deep sadness. Maybe that's why I work like a Mexican mule on a dry piece of farmland in 110-degree heat. Work takes my mind off reality. I don't talk, I don't protest, I try not to cry, and I don't use my voice to speak the truth. *Nada.* I just work.

I guess a part of me thinks that if I work hard enough I can make all the sorrow in this world go away. Of course I know I'm wrong, but it feels nice to lie to myself. Lying to myself protects me from deep despair.

Sí, entiendo La Llorona pero mas de lo que yo quiero. I understand La Llorona more than I want.

With all these heavy thoughts running through my brain, I walked through the front door of *mi casa* and headed for the dining room table so I could sit down and finish my class assignments before I had to prepare dinner, wash the dishes, and put my younger brothers to bed. Freshman year had been tough because I hadn't slept as much as I should have. This year I knew that if I got my schoolwork done earlier in the evening, I wouldn't have to stay up until all hours of *la noche* finishing assignments. Math was done, yes, but this year I had a crazy man named Mr. Wardin for World History, and he was already pounding us with giant amounts of work I didn't even hardly understand. I could already tell it would take a whole lot of effort to keep up in his class.

I parked myself down at the dining room table and opened up the eight hundred–page World History textbook. Of course, I would have done my homework somewhere else if I could have because I was sitting in the middle of the living room, which meant that I was also sitting right in the middle of all our family noise and chaos. But there was nowhere else.

The dining room table was the only place in *mi* entire *casa* where I had space to study. And sometimes I was lucky to even have that. I turned to Chapter One.

"*Sonia . . . ayúdame.*"

I closed Chapter One.

Mi ama was calling me from her favorite place in the whole wide world—her bed—hypnotized by a *telenovela*. I once tried to watch a *telenovela* with my mother so we could have a little *ama-mija* bonding time, but the story line was about a lesbian who had decided to sleep with a man for the very first time, and it turned out that the guy was her unknown twin brother, so of course she ended up getting pregnant with the incestuous baby of a long-lost sibling. Ever since that day I have thought *telenovelas* were the stupidest thing ever to hit our planet. Stupider than telesales people or government politicians, even.

Still, *mi ama* loved them. She was literally addicted, watching *telenovelas* for hours and hours every day.

In her hand she held a late notice from the gas company. The only reason she'd called me in was because she needed me to read it.

Though *mi papi* made all the money, Ama paid all the bills, and she had a special system to running the economics of our house. The first bill that came, the one that said when the money was due, would always get thrown away. Then the second notice would come telling us again that a payment was due, and she'd throw that one away also. Only the third bill, the one that said FINAL NOTICE, would get paid, and even then she'd wait until the last day before the money was actually due to pay the cash we owed. It was my mother's way of holding on to our family's fortune as long as possible before spending it.

Of course, her system resulted in lots of late fees and we'd end up having our phone, lights, water, and heat turned off all the time, but *mi ama* was convinced her schemes kept us richer than we would have been had she not figured out the secret to wealth and prosperity in America.

"*Sólo es el segundo,*" I said, handing her back the letter. Only notice number two.

"*Bueno,*" she replied, tearing up the paper. The gas bill people would have to send at least a third request if they wanted their money. I shook my head. The last time my mother screwed with the gas company, we took cold showers for eleven days.

"*Sonia . . . ayúdame,*" she said, reaching out her hands for me to help her out of bed.

I know it's not nice to think of pregnant people as fat, but *mi ama* was swelling up like a *burrito gordo*. My new brother and sister—we had already found out that Ama was carrying twins, one boy and one girl—would be children number six and seven in *la casa*. Really, they should have been eight and nine, but my mother had had two miscarriages a few years ago. We were never allowed to mention them, though. In my *familia* there were always things like that which were known to everyone but no one was ever allowed to mention. Stuff like miscarriages and homosexual relatives always got swept under the rug.

Of course, I know that giving birth to nine children sounds like a lot in the United States, but back in Mexico, it's nothing. *Mi abuelita*, my grandmother, had fourteen children, and many of them had nine to thirteen kids of their own. I have so many cousins that if we ever hold a family reunion we'll need to rent the Grand Canyon.

"*Mira*," *mi ama* instructed as we walked into the kitchen. She wanted me to take a look at a special letter she'd received in the mail. I scanned the top line.

YOU HAVE ALREADY WON 10 MILLION DOLLARS!

"*Es basura*," I said, telling her it was garbage. But *mi ama* knew all too well what the letter said. She'd seen the commercials of people who had won millions of dollars many times before from letters like these, and she wasn't about to just let me throw away her opportunity to sail on luxury yachts and drive Rolls-Royces.

"*Dime*," my mother instructed as she led me to the dining room table so I could inform her about how we could claim our prize. Ama felt one hundred percent sure that people in the United States loved to give money away for free. All she wanted was her fair share. She pushed my schools books aside.

"*Oye*, farthead," my drunkle called from his reclining position on the couch to my younger brother. My drunkle always called my younger brothers by offensive names. They loved it.

"Bring me a *cerveza*," he said in Spanish.

Miguel, though he was only eight years old, eagerly ran to the kitchen to fetch my drunkle a beer. He returned a few seconds later.

"Hey, *estúpido*," my drunkle complained when Miguel delivered him the bottle. "When you bring someone *una cerveza*, you need to open it for them."

"*Pero* I don't know how," my younger brother answered with an innocent look on his face.

"You don't know how to open a *cerveza*? What are you, some kind of retard?" my drunkle replied. "Go get the opener, ass face. I will teach you."

I raised my eyes and stared at *mi ama* with a "look." Latinos are the champions of communicating things with "looks." *Mi ama* lowered her gaze and pointed back to the **10 MILLION DOLLARS!** letter, trying to ignore what was going on between my brother and her brother, two feet behind us.

Miguel raced in and out of the kitchen, more excited to learn than at any other time in his educational history. When he handed my drunkle the bottle opener, my drunkle sat Miguel in his lap and began to teach him what he considered to be a very important life lesson.

"Now, you hold one hand around the neck, and the other hand grips the opener and . . . *¡Pssst!* . . . *¡Abierta!*"

"*¡Fantástico!*" shouted Miguel as some fizz rose out the top of the bottle. They both smiled.

"*¿Quieres?*" my drunkle then asked, wanting to know if my eight-year-old brother cared for a sip of beer.

"*¡Sí!*" shouted Miguel, eager to taste the brew.

I raised my eyes and glared at *mi ama*. She paused, then slowly turned to my drunkle.

"Ernesto . . ." *mi ama* pleaded, but she pleaded so weakly, I knew there was no way he was going to listen.

"*Relájate,*" her brother replied, telling my mother

to relax herself. "One little sip isn't going to hurt him. It'll make him a man."

Miguel eagerly reached for the bottle.

"Ernesto, *por favor*," *mi ama* repeated as my drunkle lifted the beer toward my younger brother's mouth. But my drunkle continued, completely disregarding *mi ama*.

"It's only one sip," he answered. "Besides, if it was up to you, all the men in this household would be pussies."

"Ernesto, your language."

"You see," my drunkle replied with a smile. "Here, idiot boy . . . take a sip."

I watched my eight-year-old brother raise the bottle to his lips. Not being content to merely taste the brew, he greedily began to glug. After a moment, my drunkle pulled the bottle away and grinned, proud to have passed his wisdom down from one generation to the next. Me, I wondered if this was the moment in Miguel's life that would one day lead him to become yet another brown-skinned *alcohólico*.

"*Uno más,*" Miguel said eagerly.

"No," said my drunkle, suddenly the voice of reason. "Only one."

"*Sí, uno más,*" said Miguel in a playful way as he quickly reached for the beer.

"Oops."

A look of anger flashed across my drunkle's eyes. Miguel had knocked the beer out of my drunkle's hands, spilling it everywhere.

"Sorry."

"*¡Estúpido!*" shouted my drunkle, his pants soaking wet. *BAM!* My drunkle smashed Miguel in the chest. A loud thump echoed through the room. The force of the blow knocked my brother clean off his feet, and he landed hard on his butt on the floor.

Miguel looked up. Fear filled his eyes. My drunkle began to stand slowly, meanly, angrily, then took a step toward Miguel. A tear began to form in Miguel's eyes, a tear which finally fell when my drunkle reached to unhitch his thick, leather belt.

Miguel's bottom lip started shaking as if he were standing outdoors in a short-sleeve shirt during a snowstorm. Everyone knew my drunkle was a man who firmly believed in the power of the belt, even on kids that weren't his own.

"*Es okay, es okay,*" *mi ama* said quickly, waddling to her feet. "Sonia, go clean it up," she said, trying to stand between Miguel and my drunkle before my younger brother received a ferocious beating. "*No es un problema,*" my mother repeated, pointing to the spilled beer on the floor. "Sonia will get it."

"Me?" I said.

Mi ama shot me a look.

"*¡Sonia, ve!*" she ordered.

I lowered my eyes, rose from my chair, and went to get some paper towels from the kitchen.

"And when you're in there," *mi ama* instructed, "bring your uncle another *cerveza*."

"*No hay más,*" Miguel suddenly called out, trying to be helpful. Everyone stopped and stared at my brother. It was a stupid thing to say, even if it was the truth that there was no more beer. A new wave of rage flashed across my drunkle's face. It was one thing to spill a beer. It was a totally different thing to spill the last beer.

"Don't worry, don't worry, Ernesto," said *mi ama* in an effort to calm my drunkle down. "Sonia will go to the store and buy more."

"*Pero* I have homework," I said.

"Sonia!" *mi ama* snapped as she shot me another look. This one was filled with laser beams. She turned back to my little brother. "*Es okay, Miguelito.* Go into the bedroom and play with your toy gun," she instructed, in order to get Miguel as far away from my drunkle as fast as she could. Miguel scampered away.

"Sit, Ernesto, sit. Sonia will be back soon. Ten minutes at the most."

Mi ama reached into her bra and pulled out a huge

stream of green twenty dollar bills that my father had just given her from cashing his weekly paycheck. Like the big bad wolf in Little Red Riding Hood, my drunkle's eyes got big, big, big when he saw the money.

Mi ama handed me one of the twenties. "Sit, Ernesto, sit," she repeated. "Sonia will be back soon. Ten minutes at most."

My drunkle paused, considering whether he wanted to beat the crap out of my brother or fart on the couch and wait for me to return with a fresh six-pack of *cerveza*.

"You have a lot to learn about raising kids, Maria," my drunkle finally said as he flopped onto the couch and grabbed the remote control. "Children need discipline or they grow up without values." He put his feet on the sofa, dirty shoes and all. "You're a bad mother, Maria. Your children have no respect."

"Sit, sit, watch," *mi ama* answered, trying not to pay any attention to his words. "Sonia will be back in no time at all."

My mother turned to me. "*Sonia . . . apúrate.*"

Apúrate means "hurry up" in Spanish. I looked over at my pile of schoolbooks that had been pushed aside. It would be a late *noche* after all.

chapter cinco

Some people may think it's weird that my mother would send a fifteen-year-old to buy *cerveza* at the market, but around my neighborhood, the liquor store people only care about one thing: money. They'd sell teenagers anything we asked for as long as we had the cash to pay for it. Cigarettes, condoms, rolling papers, wine: if I could shell out for it, they would sell it to me. Money, like they say, makes the world go 'round.

Too bad no one told that to the guy who had just opened Santiago's Pet Store, though. After all, the only thing he had to offer customers were pooper-scoopers, fish, and stuff like that. Didn't he know that around this part of the city tequila outsold dog cookies by about one hundred million to one? However, I love animals, so I decided to go inside and check out the new neighborhood business. Plus, hope-fully, my drunkle would be getting really thirsty back at the *casa*.

I walked up to the door of the pet store and paused. Maybe I shouldn't, I thought. I mean, there was still the beer to buy, dinner to prepare, and my younger brothers would, as usual, need help with their homework. After all, if I didn't keep them straight in school, no one would.

Yes, I thought. Best to get on with the other things I still had to do. The sooner I did, the sooner I could get back to my own schoolwork. I turned around.

Then something pulled me.

I know it sounds weird to say "something pulled me," but this was a real pull, only not by a person. Now, usually I don't believe in all that mumbo jumbo "something pulled me" stuff, but this pull was strong, almost freaky. It was as if God himself was telling me I needed to walk inside that pet store.

Two minutes after I entered, I understood why. It was love at first sight.

His green eyes sparkled with a combination of emerald and caramel, the tempting, swirling kind that tastes really good on an ice-cream sundae. His lips were thin and elegant. And oh, *mamacita*, the heat

30

that burned between us when we first looked at one another: you could have cooked *carne asada* on an outdoor griddle with all that fire. I almost had to turn away from all the *pasión*.

Suddenly, while I was staring at him, he whirled around in the other direction and began to walk away, trying to pretend that he hadn't noticed me. Obviously, he was playing hard to get. Of course, this only made me want him more. I sat there and watched his butt jiggle. For sure, there was an undeniable attraction between us.

Maybe some creatures are really meant to be together, like Adam and Eve, Wilma and Fred, Tom and Jerry. All I knew was that I instantly wanted to hug him and hold him in my arms forever. He had adorable ears, a triangle nose, small feet, and a giant lump in his stomach, as if he had swallowed a big ol' bean. That's why I decided to name him Frijolito, slang for "little bean." It was obvious that he was the runt of the litter, but this kitten was the most adorable creature I'd ever seen. It was as if Frijolito and I had known each other in a prior life.

"*¿Quieres cargarlo?*" asked a voice in Spanish, inquiring if I wanted to hold the kitty.

"*Sí,*" I answered.

The boy lifted the tiny cat out of the small kennel

and gently passed him over to me. Frijolito started to purr.

Wow, was he soft. It seemed that the muscle in his left ear wasn't strong enough to hold the point of his ear all the way up, but his whiskers were amazing, a series of straight, intersecting lines that looked as if they'd been drawn up in God's geometry class or something.

I stood there petting the kitten while he purred and purred and purred. *It's a boy, right?* I suddenly asked myself. I flipped Frijolito over, checked between his legs, and saw his two tiny little kitten balls.

Yep, he was a boy.

Once I confirmed his manhood, I flipped Frijolito back over, and he began to purr again. Holding him in my arms was the most relaxed I'd felt in almost two years.

"He likes you," said the boy who worked at the pet store. "And I think his taste is to be highly saluted."

I raised my eyes. The boy smiled. He had dark, smooth skin and glistening, white teeth. For a moment I was stunned.

Then I squinched my eyes and shot him back a hard look that said, "Dream on, *Príncipe* Charming."

As much as I liked fairy tales, I hated them too.

Especially the one about Prince Charming, the guy who comes in and saves the day, and he and the princess fall madly in love and live happily ever after. That sounds nice, but *Príncipe* Charming's a myth, total BS. Especially when it comes to Latino men. Latino men suffer from too much *machismo*. They think they're tough. They think they're cool. They think they're entitled to order a woman around just because we have a vagina. *La verdad es* they're just a bunch of mama's boys. Mama's boys who play with their penises.

Of course, I know a lot of girls my age dream about boyfriends and husbands and marriages and big wedding *fiestas*, but I think it's better not to have your heart broken, your dreams crushed, and your cherry plucked before you're even old enough to drive a car, so I do my best to stay away from them. Basically, boys are trouble. And Latino boys are the worst kind.

You know, I really wish someone would explain to me why Latino men have no problem providing the baby batter, but when it comes to everything else, so many young girls get *nada más*? No love. No support. Not even a diaper for the kids to poop in. I mean, how come they don't teach that fairy tale in elementary school, the one about the abandoned, pregnant, teenage, Hispanic welfare mom who works part-time for minimum wage, cleaning office buildings at night?

No, *Príncipe* Charming doesn't exist.

Okay, so I sound like an old maid when I say this. Plus, I like cats, which for sure means that I am going to spend the rest of my life alone. But I can't even imagine what it would be like to have too *few* people in my life. After all, my house is so filled with people, I've even learned to poop quietly, like a mouse. But at least I know one day I won't be dependent on a man to pay my bills and give me money so that if I wanted to go buy a new cordless telephone I'd have to ask permission. That's why an education isn't just about a dumb piece of paper to me. It's also about freedom and power. An education means I won't have to be any macho man's two-breasted slave. One day when I have a diploma, I will tell a man, "Wash your own dishes. And make sure you use hot water." Boys never use hot water when they wash the dishes.

Of course, *machistas* hate this idea. That's because they want their women weak. It's like it's been bred into them from birth, a tradition from the old country or something. The men go off and do what they want, not telling their wives where they are going or when they are coming home or who they are going with, while the women stay home and cook and clean and feed the kids and worry. But I am part of a new generation of Latina women, a generation that isn't going to stand for the *mierda* anymore, and I don't care if we leave all the macho men in the dust.

¡*Cabrones!*

I turned to the pet-store boy, who was smiling at me, with a burn in my eye. And I handed him back Frijolito.

Rude, I thought, and walked out.

Okay, I admit, the boy was cute. But the cute ones are always the most dangerous.

Fifteen minutes later, I bought my drunkle a six-pack of *cerveza* and headed back to *la casa*.

And no, they didn't check for ID.

chapter seis

When I showed up to my house, *¡sorpresa!* my drunkle was gone. And I bet a bunch of my mom's green twenty dollar bills were gone, too. I should have figured. It was like the phrase *pedazo de mierda* was invented just for him.

However, for all his piece-of-crapness, I had to admit my drunkle wasn't an idiot. After all, it takes a lot of smarts to continue to con your *familia* out of a place to stay, eat, sleep, and shower for most of your life without ever having had a real job.

Maybe *mi papi* was the dumb one. Not only did he work like a dog, the money he brought home to his wife always got slipped to my drunkle so that he could have a little spending cash. Of course, what he spent it on was tequila, card games, cigarillos, and *putas*. While my dad sweated like a pig, cleaning the towels of white people at a fancy sports gym, my drunkle drank, gambled, smoked, and whored away my father's *dinero*.

But hey, *es familia*, right?

I turned on the stove and got ready to prepare dinner. As usual, it took me until almost eleven to get everything finished around *la casa* before I could finally sit back down at the dining room table and begin my homework. I took a breath to clear my head and switched on my most favorite object in the whole world: my study light.

Though it was old, ugly, beat-up, and had only cost three dollars at a garage sale when the Villalobos family was evicted from their house—to me it had charm. The only problem was when I used it the drapes in our front room were so cheap people could easily see into our house from the outside. That's why I made sure never to pick my nose when studying. Or at least I picked it when my back was turned to the front window. After all, girls get boogers too.

At 12:28 a.m. I switched off my study lamp. *Finalmente*. Even though it meant I'd be getting less than five hours of sleep, I had cracked the last biology problem, finished my reflective paragraph for English class, and had done the ten end-of-chapter-questions for World History. Despite what people think about our "underperforming" school, our teachers assigned a lot of homework.

"*Muy bien, tortuguita,*" I told myself when I finally crawled under my sheets. I felt like I'd been run over by a locomotive—a locomotive that would probably hit me again tomorrow—but I knew one day my efforts would pay off. They had to. After all, that's how the story always ends for *tortuguitas*.

I was asleep before my head hit the pillow.

chapter siete

The next day, just before the first-period bell rang, Tee-Ay approached. "Yo, let me see your math stuff."

Of course I know that copying homework is what friends let other friends do in high school, but I had stayed up really late doing all my work, while I knew for a fact that Tee-Ay had been over at Constancy's house watching a movie.

She held out her hand.

"Come on, let's have it. The bell's gonna ring."

I looked at my backpack. Letting Tee-Ay get a zero on her assignment would be good for her. She'd been slipping lately anyway. Maybe it would wake her up.

She waved hi to a guy across the hall named Rickee.

"Hurry up, Sonia," she said. "I told ya, the bell's gonna ring."

I opened my mouth to say something about how she needed to do her own work. I opened my mouth to say something about how she needed to learn this stuff for herself. I opened my mouth to say something about how she needed to start working to her full potential, quit being so self-absorbed, and stop spending so much time with Constancy, because that girl's whole life was headed for trouble and Tee-Ay was going to be dragged right down with her if she didn't wake up and smell the *café con leche*.

I opened my mouth to say a whole lot of things. Tee-Ay didn't need my math homework. Tee-Ay needed someone to tell her to get her head out of her butt.

But just because I opened my mouth doesn't mean any words came out. I stood there for a moment like a person waiting for someone to pop a grape between their lips that never comes. After a moment of looking like a complete openmouthed dork-asaurus, I lowered my eyes, reached into my backpack, and passed Tee-Ay my math work.

"Finally," she said. "You move like some sort of turtle."

That afternoon I walked home feeling like a loser. Plus, I had a giant migraine. All I wanted to do was take a nap.

"Sonia . . ." cried my mother as soon as I entered through the front door. *"¡Ayúdame!"*

There was no, "How was your day?" There was no, "How are your classes?" There was no, "Did you let your best friend cheat off your math homework despite the fact that you wanted to tell her she's been acting like a real jerk lately?"

No, there was none of that. All I got was, *"¡Sonia . . . ayúdame!"* Couldn't I even have a chance to pee?

Before I knew it, I'd been sent back to the *mercado* with strict instructions to buy things like cheapie paper napkins, the kind that always fall apart in your hands and never get your fingers clean, no matter how hard you try to scrub them. But since they cost less, this is what I was told to get.

As I walked to the store I promised myself that one day, when I graduated from school and got a high-quality job, I would buy good paper napkins, the kind that really get your fingers clean. To me, nothing in the world could be worse than living your whole life using only cheapie paper napkins.

Suddenly I wanted to cry. How pathetic, I thought. I had turned into a wuss whose big dream in life was to buy good paper napkins. Could anything be more sad?

I made a left at the corner to go do the only thing

I could think of that would make me feel better. Lucky for me, the stupid rude boy was nowhere in sight.

An old man asked if he could be of help. I pointed to the little brown kitten with the lump in its tummy. I think the old man could tell that I didn't have any money to buy the kitten, but still he let me hold it. And he did it with a smile. People who work in pet stores are always so nice. Not like liquor stores, where people are mean even when you are actually going to pay for something.

Frijolito started to purr. I knew he understood me. The old man told me to take my time and went to feed some birds. I stroked the top of Frijolito's head. Two minutes of sheer, blissful silence passed.

"I knew you'd be back," said a voice, breaking the sheer, blissful silence.

"You didn't know," I snapped in return.

"I did," he said. "It's been written in the stars."

I tried to think of something clever to say that would shut him up.

"I wouldn't know about the stars," I responded. "Around here, there's too much smog to see the sky."

That should get him to leave me alone, I thought.

"That's because you need to look with heart and not your eyes," he answered with a smile.

Damn! I thought. He out-clevered me. But did *Príncipe* Charming really expect a cheesy line like that to work?

A moment passed. I didn't speak and neither did he. During the quiet I could feel him standing behind me, but I refused to turn around. I didn't want to give him the satisfaction of thinking I was interested.

Because I wasn't.

Finally I couldn't take it any longer, so I spun around and handed Frijolito back to the stupid rude boy. It was time to go.

"I greatly look forward to seeing you again," he said as I headed for the exit.

"Who's to say I'll be back?" I answered with a snippy attitude.

"Oh, you will," he replied. "It's been written."

He smiled again, and I noticed his eyes were green, like emeralds swimming in pools of clear water.

"You need to go back to astronomy class," I said without smiling back at him. "Your stars are wack."

The bell on the pet store door jingled as I left. It was cold outside. I buttoned my coat and crossed the street.

A few minutes later I found myself inside the *supermercado* with detergent, tortillas, and paper towels in my shopping cart. Of course, every product

I purchased was the cheapie kind, but I wasn't sure how they had gotten into my cart since I didn't remember shopping for them. My mind was a million miles away. No matter what I did, the stupid rude boy with eyes the color of emeralds wouldn't get out of my head.

chapter ocho

Three days later, as the water on the stove began to boil for the beans I was about to cook, I finally realized what the problem with the stupid rude boy was. He was too good looking. After all, if there is one type of boy that can't be trusted—not that any of them can be, but if there's one kind in particular—it's the good-looking kind. An ugly boy with a carved-up face and a nose where his ear should be, that kind of boy you might be able to trust. But a cute one? No way.

I told myself that no matter how much I adored Frijolito, I would not go back to the pet store. Only bad things could come of it. *La escuela* needed to be my focus, not *muchachos*.

"I knew you'd return," he said.

"I'm here for the kitten," I answered.

"I believe you," he said, completely not believing me. Cute boys like him are always so arrogant.

Without saying another word, he passed me Frijolito. We spent a moment in silence. Me and the cat, that is. I tried to put the stupid rude boy out of my brain even though he was standing right beside me, staring as if he were all googly-ga-ga in love or something. Finally he broke the silence.

"I have looked forward to seeing you more than a flower looks forward to the rain."

Why couldn't the stupid rude boy have eyes the color of puke? No one ever got seduced by eyes the color of puke.

"Tell me your name," he said.

"No," I answered. I knew I shouldn't have come.

"No is a very strange name, especially for such a beautiful girl," he responded. "Tell me, do you have a brother named Yes?"

He was making fun of me. I refused to answer.

"A sister named Up? A cousin named Down?" he continued. "Maybe you have an auntie named Maybe?" he added, smiling at me with his perfect, white teeth. "So No, is there a Yes or a Maybe in your family?"

"My name is not No," I finally shot back. And then once I'd said it, I felt like I had to say something else.

"My name is Sonia," I added, having lost the battle to withhold my name from him.

Of course that meant the next thing he would probably do was tell me his name. That's how the trouble always started.

"*Me llamo Geraldo,*" the boy said, introducing himself with a small, gracious bow of his head. "*Mucho gusto.*"

The Spanish rolled sweetly off his tongue as if he had been born of noble birth. However, it wasn't Mexican Spanish he was speaking. I could tell instantly by his accent Geraldo was Salvadoran.

"Dine with me."

"I can't."

"Lunch?"

"No."

"Breakfast?"

"I must go."

"A light snack?"

"Here," I said, passing Frijolito back to him. "I have to leave."

"Coffee? Tea? A Snickers bar with a cup of vegetable soup."

A Snickers bar with a cup of vegetable soup? I couldn't help but smile.

"You are radiant," he said when he saw the

grin on my face. "I see galaxies in your beauty."

Galaxies in my beauty? I wondered how many times *Príncipe* Charming had used that line before.

"I have to go," I said, heading for the exit. The little bells on the door jingled as it closed behind me.

When I stepped out onto the sidewalk, a chill of brisk air hit my face. Outside it was turning to winter, but I wasn't cold.

Probably because the stupid rude boy was so HOT!

Geraldo! Geraldo! Geraldo!

I floated home with my head spinning. After all, there were galaxies in my beauty.

chapter nueve

"*Ay, finalmente,*" came a voice in rapid-fire Spanish before my key was even out of the lock. "Your poor mother is stuck in bed and needs a thousand things, and you take forever to make a simple trip to *el mercado*. Such disrespect is the devil's work."

It was my aunt, Tía Luna, my mom's superfat, super religious sister. Jesus hung on her wall. Jesus hung on her neck. Jesus filled up every area of my aunt's life except her mouth. That was reserved for threats of the devil. And cupcakes.

"Just look at this house. It's as filthy as *el diablo*'s playpen," she snapped at me.

Despite the fact that she was pointing at me with an index finger so plump it looked like a wiener popping out of a hot dog bun, I had to admit Tía Luna was right. There was a giant mess. Across the coffee table were potato chip crumbs, two cherry soda cans, and a half-eaten bag of imitation Oreo cookies, the cheapie kind that pretended they were the same as real Oreo cookies but tasted fakely different.

Tía Luna leaned forward, grabbed three black-and-white cheapie cookie sandwiches, and started plopping them into her mouth.

"You need to learn the ways of the old country," she said as she gobbled down the round little treats. "Or the devil is going to roast your soul in the fires of eternal damnation."

"You tell her, Tía," chirped in Rodrigo as he reclined on the couch, watching Speedy Gonzales cartoons. "The devil's gonna get her."

While I always had about ten thousand chores to get done, my older brother, Rodrigo, pretty much went through life as a lazy, do-nothing, sit-on-the-sofa-and-play-video-games loser. He had failed every class he'd ever taken since seventh grade (including PE), dropped out of high school after ninth grade, and aside from an occasional part-time job from which he'd get fired within two weeks of being hired, he pretty much spent his life reinforcing negative stereotypes about Mexicans being lazy, uneducated, good-for-nothing, brown-skinned troublemakers.

Not that he and I didn't get along or anything.

"Don't you give him the devil's eye," Tía Luna said to me with black cookie-crumb dust covering her teeth. "Rodrigo's a good boy, but *el diablo*'s schemes hold men like him back in this country," she said, crossing herself.

Funny, I thought it was all the *mota* Rodrigo smoked that held him back. One look at his red eyes, and all the munchies lying everywhere, should have told my aunt that Rodrigo was stoned out of his head. But of course it didn't. In me, Tía Luna saw the devil. In Rodrigo, she saw a martyred saint.

And people wondered why I stopped going to church.

"Amen," said Tía Luna after she crossed herself again and mumbled some prayers for Rodrigo. Then she grabbed three more cookies. Praying always inspired her appetite.

"Does Jesus got my back, Tía?" asked Rodrigo with red, glossy eyes.

"Jesus loves you, Rodrigo," Tía Luna answered. "Jesus loves everyone. But the devil loves, too, and he especially loves the sinners," my aunt said, looking at me with a menacing glare. "Give up your sinful ways, Sonia, before the fires of Satan melt your flesh like shredded cheese on top of an *enchilada a la diabla*." Slowly she put another fake Oreo in her mouth. The cookie disappeared like a quarter being sucked into a sideways slot machine.

I had to admit, part of me wanted to give up all of my responsibilities and sit on the couch smoking weed and eating potato chips all day like Rodrigo, too. Well, not smoking pot, because I didn't do drugs, but eating chocolate-chip cookies while watching old black-and-white movies all day didn't sound so bad. I like black-and-white movies, especially the love stories.

Of course, whenever I thought like this, the words of my father would ring through my ears. "*Mija*, do not stoop to that level."

Then, a moment later another voice rang out.

"*Sonia . . . ayúdame.*"

I paused before responding. Silence hung in the air as both Tía Luna and Rodrigo waited for me to get up and see what my mother wanted. I rolled my eyes. Now what, I thought. I just got home.

"*Oye, Sonia, ayuda a tu ama . . .*" Rodrigo ordered me to go help our mother before she called out again. "*Y tengo hambre. ¿Cuándo comemos?*" he added with an attitude of "Can you hurry up and get dinner on the table too?"

I scowled at *mi hermano*. Tía Luna, seeing my look of anger shook her head with so much disapproval that the fat on her neck started to jiggle like a holiday turkey before it goes to the chopping block.

"I pray the devil doesn't burn you too long, Sonia," Tía Luna said, as if she were being compassionate. "But once he has you in his flames, he'll show no mercy."

I rolled my eyes, put down the cheapie paper towels, and headed for the bedroom. Even inside my own house, I was always the outsider.

"*¿Tía, te gusta Speedy González?*" my brother asked, inquiring if my aunt liked the mouse in the cartoon he was watching.

"I don't know, *mijo*," answered my aunt as she reached for the last remaining cookie in the bag. "Does he reject Satan?"

It turned out that all *mi ama* wanted from me was to read a simple **30 DAY NOTICE OF RENTAL PRICE INCREASE** from the white man who owned our house. However, when she asked me to do this, I wanted to EXPLODE!

It wasn't reading the letter that bothered me. It was only going to take me *dos minutos* to do that and explain to her that our rent was being increased by four percent, due at the beginning of next month. (I only wished all my chores took this long.) What made me so angry was the fact that *mi ama* had been in this country for almost sixteen years and still knew practically no English. *Mi papi*, ever since the day he got here, had worked two or three jobs and still had made the time to learn enough of the language so that he could at least hold some kind of conversation with a *gabacho*, but *mi ama*, with all her free time, still knew almost nothing.

Of course, if *telenovelas* were in English, she'd have spoken like William Shakespeare.

I looked at the piece of paper and burned on the inside. A minute later, Tía Luna walked in the bedroom and informed us that she'd be staying for dinner. No, she didn't ask, she'd just simply invited herself. And since my fat aunt always ate the equivalent of three Jesus Christs and all of the apostles combined, there wouldn't be enough food for the evening meal unless someone went to the market.

That someone would, of course, be me.

Mi ama crumpled up the letter from the landlord. After all, it was only the first notice. Then she turned to tell me what to buy for dinner. It seemed I'd be cooking tortilla soup and *arroz con pollo*. That's when I snapped.

"*Sonia, cuando vayas al mercado, no te olvides traer . . .*"

"No!" I said, before she finished her sentence.

Mi ama and Tía Luna froze.

"*¿Cómo?*" asked *mi ama*.

There was a long pause. I didn't answer. After another moment, she began again.

"*Escúchame, Sonia. Cuando vayas al mercado, compras . . .*"

"I said, No," I replied in English. "I have homework." I knew that answering in *inglés* would only make her more upset, but I also knew that she understood every single damn word I was saying.

"Let someone else do something for a change," I continued. "You only take advantage of me because I'm a girl."

With that I headed for the door.

"*Ay, Dios mío,*" Tía Luna said in Spanish. "Satan prevents her from knowing the sacrifices you've made for her. I'll pray for her, Maria, but I fear your daughter is going to be boiled in the oils of hell and served like *papas fritas* to the devil with a *hamburguesa.*"

I stopped, turned, and glared at Tía Luna. "Is that before or after I clean up the sticky stuff off the counters Rodrigo spilled in the kitchen?"

Tía Luna gasped in horror.

"*¡Al Diablo!*" she said, recoiling back.

I slammed the door behind me, plopped myself down at the dining room table, and turned on my study light.

No, it wasn't the devil that made me do what I did. It was the *tortuguita*, and at that moment I swore to myself that even if it took me a thousand years, I would never turn into my mother. Never! The United States was all about opportunity, and I wasn't going to let anyone steal mine. Especially not *mi familia*.

Cross my heart and hope to die.

That night we ate El Pollo Loco for dinner. In total silence.

chapter diez

I focused on school. Of course, I still did my chores around *mi casa*, but not at the expense of my homework and classes. For the next two weeks we ate more takeout than ever before. McDonald's, Burger King, KFC, everything. We even ate Taco Bell, the most unMexican Mexican food there is.

A week later I also told Tee-Ay that she was being cut off from any more of my homework. I told her she needed to learn math for herself, and I shut her down cold turkey just like a *mujer* shuts off the love machine from *un hombre* who gets caught with *una Sancha*.

At first I could tell Tee-Ay didn't think I was serious, but soon she learned. I didn't give her any more assignments for the entire year. *¡Nada!*

Okay, *sí*, I felt guilty that I wasn't cooking and

cleaning every night, like Cinderella Rodriguez, but my grades were getting better, and that's what really mattered. Plus, I knew that my diploma was the only real way for me to get out and live a good life in America, and I was so determined to earn one that I even made the decision of no more Frijolito. While I was going to miss the kitten, I couldn't risk having the stupid rude boy distract me from my goals. He'd really fuzzed up my brain for a few days, and I didn't have time for that anymore. Classes were most important, then chores around the house to help *mi ama*. After all, she was pregnant with twins and I couldn't just turn into my loser brother Rodrigo all of a sudden. That wouldn't have been right. But boys were *absolutamente* out of the picture for me.

I walked home from school on the last day of the first quarter with my report card saying I had earned a 3.23 GPA. For the first time in a long while I felt proud of myself. I had won a family battle.

Pero, as I soon learned, just because I had won a battle didn't mean I had won the war.

It started with the mattress on the floor. Living with so many brothers, I'd just thought they had tossed everything on the floor in the bedroom because they were playing battle combat or something. You know how stupid boys can be. Then I heard a burp.

Two seconds later, the foul, nasty stink of booze-breath floated through the air. I didn't have to turn around to know who it was.

"*Estoy aquí,*" said my drunkle, his voice low and serious. I spinned around and saw that he had a cut over his right eye, a gash that looked a few days old, with dried blood crusted over it.

"*Haz la cama,*" he told me, instructing me to fix up the bed. Obviously, he'd be staying. For how long, I did not know.

I began to do what he said. He watched from the doorway.

As I made up the room, I realized it wasn't too hard to figure out that my drunkle was flat broke, had done something really bad, and was most likely a wanted man. By who, I did not know, but the tone in his voice made it clear he'd be here for a while. Indefinitely, perhaps.

And how could we say no? After all, *somos familia.* We're family.

I tossed a clean sheet over the mattress. My drunkle had decided to take Rodrigo's bed, which meant Rodrigo would take Oscar's bed, and Oscar would take Miguel's bed. Miguel would end up sleeping on the floor because he had no one younger than him to boot from bed except Hernando, but since Hernando was only two years old and still sleeping in a crib, Miguel would be on the ground. The youngest always got screwed when it came to stuff like this.

I reached over to tuck in the sheets at the far corner.

"It'll be good for you to have a man around, with your father away so much," my drunkle said as I bent over to fix the sheets. "A man that can watch over you as you develop and mature."

A cold chill swept over my body, and the hair on my neck began to rise. I didn't dare turn around, but I could feel my drunkle's red, bloodshot eyes watching me, staring at me, looking me over, up and down, side to side.

"*Dime, ¿cuántos años tienes?*" my drunkle asked, wanting me to remind him how old I was. I paused.

I tucked in the last corner of the bedsheet, not quite knowing what to do. Then I stood and turned to face him. Though he was family, my stomach fluttered with fear.

I opened my mouth. My throat felt swollen. No words came out of my lips.

My drunkle looked me in the eye. Then he squinted and gazed down at my breasts.

"*Sonia . . .*" a voice suddenly called. "*Ayúdame.*" We both looked up.

It was the first time in my life I had ever been glad to hear those words. I lowered my head and took a step forward to exit the bedroom and go help *mi ama*. My drunkle, however, blocked the doorway.

He didn't move.

I waited.

He still didn't move.

I waited some more.

"*Con permiso, Tío,*" I finally said.

He looked at me long and hard. I remained staring at the floor.

"*Sonia . . .*" *mi ama* called again. Another moment passed. Finally, my drunkle stepped aside.

"*Ve . . .*" he said, granting me permission to leave. But he didn't clear from the doorway. Instead he turned to the side, making it so that I had to squeeze past him to get out. "*Pase.*"

I paused. There was no way for me to exit other than to try and slide past him. I turned sideways. My breasts rubbed against him. For a moment I was entirely pressed against his body. He stunk of body odor. Two seconds later I was out in the hall, and a few steps after that, inside *mi ama*'s bedroom.

"*¿Qué te pasa?*" she asked in an annoyed voice when I walked in, wondering what had taken me so long. I didn't answer.

"*Dígame,*" she said, sensing that something wasn't quite right. I must have been white as a *gabacho* from Wisconsin. She reached for the remote control and lowered the volume on the television set.

"*¿Qué te pasa?*" she asked again.

"*Nada,*" I replied in a barely audible voice. Then my drunkle appeared.

"*Necesitamos otro papel para el baño, María. Este papel está muy escamoso. Por qué siempre tienes que comprar el más chafa?*"

My mother raised her eyes and stared at her brother, wondering where he had come from so quickly to complain about the cheap toilet paper she always purchased. But there was only one place he could have come from, in the other bedroom with me. I watched as *mi ama* tried to put two and two together.

Yet some people are no good at math. Or maybe it's just that they don't really try.

"*Sí, voy a comprar otro,*" Ama answered, explaining to her brother that she'd buy new toilet paper the next day.

"*Y jabón,*" my drunkle added. "The lavender kind. I like lavender soap."

His order for bathroom supplies given, my drunkle scratched his stomach and walked away.

I raised my eyes and looked at *mi ama*. She looked back as if she were studying me. For a moment we did not speak.

But we did. A million words passed between us. However, they were the kind of words that move from one person to the other in total silence. They were words *mi ama* did not, or chose not, to acknowledge. She didn't want to see what she just saw, so instead she looked down and reached into her bra.

"*Aquí está el dinero para el mercado. Escucha, Sonia, necesitamos . . .*"

Yes, I could have said something, but at the time I thought it would have been pointless. And probably, *mi ama* wouldn't have believed me anyway, thinking it was just some sort of "thing" I had made up so I wouldn't have to do more work around the house, or something like that. She knew I had never liked her brother. Talking to her would have been stupid.

But talking to *mi papi* would be smart. After all, he was the true man of this house, even if he wasn't around very much because he worked all the time. I stayed up until 12:45 that night, waiting for him to come home. When I heard his key in the lock, I rushed to the door and almost tackled him.

"*¿Qué te pasa, mija?*" my father asked in great

surprise as I squeezed him as hard as I could before he had even finished entering.

I had planned to tell *mi papi* the truth. Everything. But then, while I was squeezing him and feeling the cold zipper of his jacket pressing up against my cheek, it occurred to me that while *mi papi* was a calm, reasonable man on the surface, deep down he was a person with great pride, and if he found out what I was about to tell him, regarding my drunkle, he would have killed him. Literally, he would have killed him. *Mi papi* would have murdered my drunkle right on the spot and would not have cared one bit about the consequences. Of course, that would mean he'd go to jail for the rest of his life.

And where would that leave the rest of the *familia*? Who would support us? Rodrigo? I doubted it. My younger brothers? They weren't even old enough to deliver newspapers. Me? I didn't stand a chance.

Plus, *mi ama* still had two more babies yet to come.

The more I thought about it, the more I realized what the consequences of my words would be. Losing *mi papi* would devastate the entire family. Murder. Jail. Scandal. Homelessness. Poverty. Our lives would fall down like dominoes.

And then I realized that my drunkle hadn't really done anything. And I could avoid him. I could stay on this side of the house when he was on that side and I could make sure that the bathroom door was always locked and that we were never alone in the same room together.

There were a million things I could do, a million things that could prevent our *familia* from losing Papi forever.

I couldn't handle losing *mi papi* forever. He was the best person in the whole world and I didn't want him to go to jail because of me. I squeezed him even tighter as tears streamed down my face.

"*Mija, dime ¿qué pasa?*" he asked again, growing more concerned.

"I just missed you, Papi," I said in Spanish. "I missed you so much. Promise me we're not going to lose you, Papi. Tell me we're not going to lose you," I said as more tears continued to flow.

He smiled with a warmth that filled my heart like a hot bowl of tortilla soup on a cold winter night. "You're not going to lose me, *mija*. You're not going to lose me at all." He hugged me close. "Besides, what would I ever do without my little *tortuguita*?" he added with a grin.

I squeezed *mi papi* again and thanked God in

heaven above that he allowed me the honor of being my father's daughter. And just like that I felt good about my decision. If I had said something, everyone would lose. But if I kept quiet and followed my plan, things would work out. I would work things out. I would work things out for the good of the *familia*. All I had to do was be smart. Things always worked themselves out for the *tortuguitas*. Just read the fairy tales. The *tortuguitas* always win.

My tears began to dry up.

"*Mija*," my father asked, seeing that I was calming down. "*¿Qué piensas sobre un champurrado?*" A smile filled my face. Though it was a school night, it would be a wonderful treat to stay up even later and make my father a cup of delicious hot chocolate, Mexican style. Besides, I made the best *champurrado* in Los Angeles, going step by step from scratch just like they did in the old country. I rushed to the kitchen with excitement. *Mi papi* followed right behind.

First I combined the *leche* and the water while mixing in *masa y harina* flour until everything was smooth. Then I added in a touch of sugar and a dash of salt as I brought the liquid to a boil. Once boiling, I lowered the heat and stirred, melting in the delicious bricks of chocolate at a slow, even pace. But I didn't just melt the bricks into the *champurrado*. I talked to

66

the chocolate. In my opinion, that was the key to getting all of the real flavor out of them. You had to whisper to them. Speak to them. Tell them kind words and make them feel as if they were being gently treated, like a little baby who was just about to fall asleep in your arms after a warm bath. Then, after everything was blended perfectly together and the liquid was piping hot, I spooned out a cup of delicious *champurrado* for *mi papi*. And one for me too. (Of course I had to have one.) Then, as I topped off *mi papi*'s cup with a spoonful of extra froth, I realized I hadn't just made a wonderful cup of *champurrado* for *mi papi*, I had made a cup of love.

"*¿Te gusta, Papi?*" I asked with hope in my voice after he took his first sip.

"Mmm," he said with a nod of his head. "Mmm."

Mi papi wasn't a talkative man, but his "Mmm" said it all. It was like he was saying that working seventeen hours a day was worth every bit of effort, energy, and sweat, because at the end of his day he was a man who got to come home and enjoy a cup of hot *champurrado* with his little *tortuguita*.

We sat there for a long time as I chatted with *mi papi* about my hopes and dreams once I graduated from high school. I told him all about the ways I'd help the family, about the ways I'd be a role model to my younger brothers and the new twins. About the ways I would one day make him very proud.

"*Mija,*" he said as if he were informing me of the most obvious fact in the world, "I'm already very proud." Then he drank the last sip of his *champurrado* and smiled with deep satisfaction. It wasn't until after 1:30 in the morning when we finally went to bed.

"*Buenas noches, Sonia,*" he said. His thick, black mustache tickled my cheek when he kissed me goodnight, just like when I was a little girl.

"*Buenas noches, Papi,*" I answered, kissing him back.

My drunkle, of course, still had not returned to *la casa* from the local bars. The last thing I did before I went to bed was put a booger on his pillow.

chapter once

As I watched fat Tía Luna stuffing chorizo into her mouth like one of those walruses gobbling dead fish at the zoo, I realized the *telenovela*-size shame a scandal with my drunkle would have brought down on every Rodriguez this side of Nogales, if I had opened my mouth. Latinos love gossip more than they like big hats or rosary beads, and what could be more juicy than the conceited daughter of Alfredo Rodriguez falsely accusing her *tío* of being a rapist? Most of my family members thought I was stuck up and conceited anyway. Personally, I didn't think this was true, but being the good student, the dutiful daughter, and the one who planned on graduating from school without getting pregnant, addicted to drugs, or caught having sex with a black man always made other family members jealous of me.

How come when a person tries to do good so many people try to bring them down? Even in my own *familia*. One thing was *segura*, though, if I had been a boy, it would have been different.

The plan to stay clear of my drunkle worked great. For weeks I had pretty much been able to avoid being alone with him without any problems, mostly because we had so many people living under one roof and someone was almost always home. Besides, he was always *bebido*, and it's just not that hard to avoid someone who stumbles around all the time due to tequila.

"Tsk, tsk, tsk," said Tía Luna, sucking on her teeth when she saw her brother lying bombed out on our floor at 3:20 in the afternoon. "The devil has him in his grips. We must do something."

She reached for more chorizo. I could tell by the way Tía Luna was gobbling down fatty chunks of pig meat that a plan was brewing in her head. On the inside, I grew excited. Of course, on the outside I couldn't show it, and had to simply continue to sit at the dining room table doing my homework under the light of my study lamp, but it felt good to know that something big was being planned for my drunkle. Whenever Tía Luna got that look in her eye about a family member, something big always happened. Something big and unpleasant.

Maybe she'd have my drunkle move in with her instead of us, to get more Jesus in his life. Maybe she'd take him to an Alcoholics Anonymous meeting and make him say, "Hi, my name is Ernesto, and I am a mean and nasty drunk." Of course, he could also say, "I am a liar, cheater, pervert, and all-around scum-sucking dirtbag." (I wonder if they have meetings for each of those things as well?) Maybe she'd just bring a priest over to do an exorcism, realize my drunkle was far too possessed by Satan for regular means, and shove a hot poker three feet up his butt in the name of Christ the Savior.

No matter what was cooking inside that little birdhouse of a brain my aunt possessed, I knew something bad was going to come out of it for my drunkle. And something bad for my drunkle was, of course, something good for me.

"He'll be forty years old next week," my aunt said with a serious look on her face.

"*Sí*, Ernesto is turning into *un viejo*," answered *mi ama* in Spanish.

"I know what we must do," my aunt finally announced. I leaned forward to listen. This was going to be good. "We'll throw him a birthday party."

"*¿Qué?*" I said.

"A birthday party, a grand fortieth fiesta to

celebrate this important milestone in his life."

"That's the stupidest idea I've ever heard of," I said.

My aunt scowled at me. "I'll pretend the devil didn't make you say that."

I lowered my eyes and looked back at my schoolwork.

"A great expression of our love will show his heart the way to Jesus," Tía Luna explained. "We'll invite everyone. The cousins, his *compadres*, the whole neighborhood. It will be a day to honor him unlike any other day he's ever known."

"*Pero* his birthday is Saturday," said *mi ama*, concerned that there wouldn't be enough time to properly host a party for what could easily be ninety to a hundred people.

"Not to worry, everyone will contribute. Food, cake, *cervezas*," assured my aunt. "A fiesta like this is just what he needs to show him the goodness of the Lord."

And just like that it was settled. On Saturday night a gigantic fortieth birthday party was going to be thrown to get my drunkle to give up his alcoholic ways. The fact that we were doing it by giving him a party that served alcohol didn't seem to bother anyone a bit.

Of course, I was sure that if my drunkle knew of this big party being planned in his honor, he would have said thank you; but since he was lying half conscious on the floor in front of everyone, the only sound he was able to make was a fart.

Initially I was scared that I would have to do everything for this party all by myself, but Tía Luna took a moment to assure me that this wouldn't be the case, that everyone would contribute.

"Everything will be taken care of, Sonia. All you'll need to do is make the tamales."

Oh, that was all, huh? Just the tamales. Why didn't she ask me to build a barn so we could give him a horse, too?

"Besides, your mother and I will help you with them. It will be quality *mujeres* time for us."

To this day I still don't know why I believed her. Guess who missed the next three days of school?

If a person watches the few movies they actually do make about Latinos, they always show the women in the kitchen sharing the joy of making tamales while smiling, laughing, and bonding in a way that passes wisdom down from one generation to the next. That's why I hate Hollywood; it's nothing like reality. Making tamales is a giant pain in the ass.

First you make the dough. The *masa*, the chicken

broth, the mixing of the lard until it's all fluffy. I hate lard. And I hate making it fluffy. And I hate combining everything together afterward and then adding in all the seasonings. Making leather shoes for two hundred feet would be easier.

After a whole day of slave labor in the kitchen, I had dough. Big deal. Later that night I did homework.

Day two started with chopping. Chopping chiles. Chopping tomatoes. Chopping onions, chopping garlic, chopping jalapeño peppers. *Mi ama*, knowing how hard it was to chop so much food for so many tamales, finally came into the kitchen to help. That was nice of her. But after being on her feet for twenty minutes, she told me that her ankles had started to swell due to the pregnancy, and she explained how *el doctor* didn't really want her on her feet, so she went back to watching *telenovelas* in the bedroom.

I think she chopped a few carrots, though, but I wasn't sure because she brought them back into her room to snack on. The only break I took was for lunch. To make my mother's lunch. After all, pregnant women need to eat, don't they?

Of course, Tía Luna was a total no-show. She was probably off buying little crucifix candleholders for decorations, or something like that.

I was so behind schedule by the second afternoon

that I had to use store-bought chile sauce. You've heard of the seven deadly sins according to the Bible? Well, the eighth sin in *mi cultura* is using store-bought ingredients for homemade tamales. However, I didn't care. If it hadn't been for jarred chile sauce, I wouldn't have finished until my drunkle's four hundredth birthday.

Then came the husks. Sorting, soaking, patting them dry, spreading the dough, filling the tamale, folding the tamale, and finally, tying the tamale. By tamale seventeen, my wrists hurt. By tamale thirty-six, my elbow ached. By tamale fifty-one my arms, neck, shoulders, and forearms were in such burning pain that I was ready to sue my mother for causing carpal tamale syndrome. Then *mi papi* walked in. Needless to say, I wasn't in the best of moods.

"Tamales," he said in an upbeat voice. "Reminds me of your *abuelita*. Her tamales are made with magic."

"Well, unlike Grandma's, these are made with Old El Paso," I answered rudely. Sweat dribbled from my temple. We sat there in silence for a minute.

I realized I had been nasty to my father. There was no need. *Mi papi* worked this hard for us all the time.

"What are you doing home?" I asked in voice that tried to sound nicer.

"*Navidad número dos*," he answered. Christmas number two, *Navidad número dos*, was a little joke we had about my father's work schedule. He only got two holidays a year off from the gym where he cleaned locker room towels from 5:30 to 11:30, six nights a week. The first was Christmas, *Navidad* number one. The second day off was when they waxed the racquetball courts. Once a year the gym would close half a day early so that the racquetball courts could be buffed and shined to a nice polish for all the white people who played on them. We called this Christmas number two.

I wished he would have at least gotten New Year's off, but the gym was always open for the fat people with new resolutions and the crazy work-out freaks who had no life beyond exercise and organic foods. As *mi papi* said, January was always the busiest month because of all the plumpies trying to lose weight. But by February things slowed down a lot for him. I guess they all went back to eating doughnuts for dinner again.

I spread, filled, folded, and tied another tamale. My hair stuck to my neck from perspiration. I looked at the pile of food with anger. Only in *mi cultura* could a person waste so much time on one meal.

Mi papi stared at me in a thoughtful way. I bet I

looked like a fifty-year-old woman to him—and I didn't care.

"*Vamos,*" he said suddenly.

"*No puedo, Papi,*" I responded as I looked over at the mounds of food yet to be prepared. Even though I had no idea where he wanted to go, I knew I couldn't join him.

"*Anda, vamos,*" he said more forcefully. "*Quiero una nieve de fresa.*" I stopped mid-tamale. Strawberry ice cream, Spanish style, was my absolute favorite in the whole world. To me there was nothing more delicious on the planet. *Mi papi* knew this was my weakness.

"*No puedo, Papi,*" I said again softly, though it certainly was nice of him to offer. "But really, I can't." There was still so much more to do before tomorrow.

"*Sí puedes,*" he insisted, taking the tamale I was about to fill. "*Quiero una nieve de fresa,*" he repeated in a determined voice and pulled me by my arm out of the kitchen. There was no fighting him. *Mi papi* had a grip that could crush a metal pipe, and I was so tired that before I could even resist, we were in the living room, where Rodrigo and my drunkle were watching a *fútbol* game on TV.

"*¿A dónde van?*" asked my brother, wanting to know where we were going. I'm sure he would have loved us to bring him a *nieve de limón* with chocolate chips on top. That was his favorite. And of course my drunkle would eat some ice cream. Usually he liked mango. Plus, my brothers in the back of the house and *Ama*, everybody loved *nieve*, no matter what the flavor. Going on an ice cream run would make the whole house happy.

"*Regresaremos,*" said *mi papi*, not directly answering Rodrigo but instead telling him in a very clear tone something that meant "We'll be back, and it's none of your hot-damn business where we're going." My drunkle's eyes looked away from the TV and scanned over to *mi papi*. A moment later, and without a word, my drunkle's gaze returned to the television set. He didn't dare question my father. There was only one rooster in this henhouse, that was for sure. Rodrigo took the hint as well and quietly went back to watching the game. As it happens, it was the third *fútbol* game in a row, a special "never-get-off-the-couch triple-header."

Mi papi turned to me. "*¿Lista?*" he asked, wanting to know if I was ready.

Screw it, I thought, and took off my apron. I hadn't even put any of the ingredients in the kitchen away.

"*Sí, quiero ir,*" I answered. I slipped on my shoes and took a step toward the door.

"*Sonia . . .*" my mother's voice suddenly called from the bedroom. I stopped and began to turn, but my father quickly hurried me out of the house and closed the door before she could yell, "*Ayúdame.*"

I looked at him with curiosity. *What if she really needs something?*

"Mmm, *nieve de fresa,*" he said, looking at me with a small, mischievous smile. A moment later we were walking down the street. *Papi* wasn't concerned about *mi ama.* She'd live, he figured.

When I was a little girl, *Papi* and I used to go for Spanish ice cream all the time. And we always held hands. Our private walks were some of the most happy memories I ever had. Of course, when you grow up and you're a teenager, it's not really that cool to walk down the street holding hands with your father, but right then I didn't care. I slipped my hand into his, and we made our way down the sidewalk. Holding hands with *mi papi* didn't make me feel ashamed. In fact, I couldn't have been more proud if my father had been the first Mexican on the moon.

To me, *mi papi* represented everything a real Latino should be. He was honest, hardworking, caring, and made sacrifices for his *familia* without calling attention to himself and without ever asking for anything in return. He didn't drink, smoke, lie, or complain. He even paid his taxes. Of course, he had to use a fake social security number to pay them, and the government had no way of giving him credit for his tax contributions, but *mi papi* felt it was the right thing to do since his kids went to American schools, his wife rode on American buses, and his feet walked on American streets. Technically, because *mi papi* was illegal, the government really shouldn't have kept his money. After all, it wasn't being properly and legally collected by them.

But of course they did. For some reason, his check to the IRS always got cashed.

Hand in hand we turned a corner and made our way down the street. I looked up and saw danger.

A few *cholos* were hanging out on the sidewalk, some scary-looking gangsta teens with shaved heads and long white T-shirts. Around my neighborhood the police had very little control of the youth, and in many ways, *cholos* ruled the community. But my father paid them no mind and simply said *"Buenas"* as we passed. If I had been alone, I would have been terrified of these four boys with tattooed necks and baggy pants. But walking along with *mi papi* and seeing the way he greeted them, suddenly I wasn't afraid at all.

"Buenas," one of the *cholos* said, nodding his

head in return. Though Latino gangstas don't respect much, they do respect a hardworking family man. We passed without a problem.

Mi papi gets labels put on him by United States society, but I don't see how he is any different from the Pilgrims I studied in history class. The Pilgrims came to America searching for opportunity. So did he. The Pilgrims worked hard and made positive contributions to the nation. So does he. The Pilgrims tried to live a decent lifestyle. So does he. After all, it's not like the Pilgrims had papers. And look at what they did to the Indians when they got here. By comparison, Latinos like *mi papi* are a bunch of fluffy soft lambs.

What it really comes down to, and what *gabachos* don't want to hear, is that white people are hypocrites. They want their lettuce picked, their houses cleaned, and their gym towels washed, but they don't want to give the people who do these things a good salary or job benefits. They make big money off cheap, immigrant labor like *mi papi*, and if the Hispanics weren't here to do these jobs, who would do them? The whites? Yeah, right. The blacks? They might clean a few sauna towels, but do you really see them out in the fields picking fruit? I doubt it. It reminds them too much of slavery and picking cotton. Would the Asians do it? Possibly yes, possibly no, but let's face it, a salad isn't a salad without a Mexican.

And we all know how white people love their salads. Could you imagine the *gringa* ladies without them? *Ay*, there'd be a revolution.

In the back of their minds, maybe white people are scared because they know the day of the Latino in America is coming. We may be a slow people, and it may take another five or ten or twenty or fifty years, but one day, the Latino voice in America will be heard. And when it is, it will be loud. There are just too many of us.

However, my guess is that our voice will probably be first spoken by Latinas. Our men are proving to be too weak in this country. Not all of them, but too many of them love alcohol, drugs, violence, and laziness way too much, and it keeps our whole culture down. But now there is a new generation of Hispanic ladies. In a way, this has been our first chance in history. Birth control, bilingualism, and bachelor's degrees—the three B's, are giving us power.

Watch out, America, here come the Latinas!

Walking along with *mi papi*, I grew excited about my future. We got to the ice-cream shop and ordered.

"*Dos, por favor,*" said *mi papi*, pointing to the flavor we wanted. "*Grande.*" I smiled. We'd each have our own large.

The lady filled our order, and *mi papi* paid with a ten dollar bill. Not being able to wait once the lady put our order on the counter, I grabbed a white plastic spoon and took a big bite. Mmm! As the taste hit my tongue, my body melted. Did I mention how much I LOVE *nieve de fresa*?

Then I saw *mi papi*. He wasn't eating. Something was wrong.

Instead of taking a bite of his ice cream, *mi papi* stared at the change that had been given to him by the lady behind the counter. It wasn't correct. I watched him recount the money two times as the lady who served us walked away. Papi paused and recounted it again. This time I counted it with him. The lady had mistakenly given *mi papi* change for a twenty dollar bill instead of a ten.

I smiled. It was a good break for *mi papi*. He worked so hard for his money that free ice cream and a little extra cash never hurt. After all, if anyone deserved it, he did.

"*Discúlpeme,*" my father then called out to the ice-cream lady.

No, Papi, keep it, I thought. The lady walked back over.

I stood there and watched as *mi papi* explained that she had made a mistake and had overchanged us.

The lady looked at the money *mi papi* held in his outstretched palm, and her cheeks grew red.

"*Ay,*" the lady said. "*Muchas gracias, señor.*"

"*De nada,*" answered *mi papi* as he handed her back the extra money. A moment later we walked outside and sat down at an outdoor table. *Mi papi* dug his spoon into the ice cream and took a big bite. I saw satisfaction come to his face.

I stared at him. He seemed to know why.

"Do not stoop to that level, *mija,*" he said to me in a simple voice. "You must always remember, do not stoop to that level." It was as if it had never been a question for him about giving back the money to the lady. Then he took a second bite of his *nieve de fresa.* "Mmm," he said. "*Está buena.*"

I smiled. Spanish ice cream really was the best.

After walking around and doing a whole lot of nothing for another hour, we returned home. Rodrigo was still on the couch, my drunkle had gone out, my younger brothers were running around playing championship wrestling, trying to kill one another, and *mi ama* was standing in the kitchen in the midst of a huge, unfinished pile of tamales. She opened her mouth to say something.

Then she didn't. I think the look in *mi papi*'s eyes scared her off. A moment later my father went to the sink, rolled up his shirtsleeves, and began to wash up.

"Now, let's make some tamales," he said.

"*Papi, no,*" I said. "Go watch the game with Rodrigo. It's your night off, and I know you love *fútbol*. I'll finish," I said.

Mi papi ignored me and glared at *mi ama*. "Please pass me that spoon," he said. *Mi ama* lowered her eyes, did as she was asked, and passed my father the spoon. A moment later she too went to the sink and started washing her hands.

The three of us finished making the rest of the tamales in about forty minutes. However, I can't say we talked that much. At least not verbally.

chapter doce

On Saturday morning I began steaming the tamales. The good news was that since it was Saturday, I didn't have to miss any *escuela* to cook them. The bad news was I had to wake up at 5:00 a.m. in order to make sure everything was prepared in time for the party. By 6:30 p.m. I had prepared enough tamales to feed an invading Latino army.

Five people showed up to the "grand fiesta." I guess my drunkle wasn't the most popular guy in town. It wasn't long before Tía Luna started in on me.

"I bet you used jarred sauce, didn't you?" she asked as she stuffed a forkful of food into her mouth.

I didn't answer.

"That's what I thought," she continued. "A white girl with an amputated arm could have made better food."

Tía Luna's realization that her brother's party was an absolute failure triggered in her a deep urge to eat, and even though she said she didn't like the tamales, she began plugging them into her Jesus hole as if her mouth were the bottom of a leaky boat and tamales were the pieces of cork that would plug it and save her life.

"Sonia needs to learn the ways of the old country," she said to my mother between snorts and chews. "A woman who can't make tamales is a woman with problems of the heart. She needs to see Abuelita."

Oh, here we go again, I thought. More talk about how I needed to learn the ways of being a "real" Latina woman from my legendary grandmother, Abuelita, the keeper of all wisdom.

Mi ama contemplated her words. Me, I just hoped she didn't contemplate them too seriously. I hadn't been to the part of Mexico where Abuelita lived since I was two years old. They didn't even have indoor bathrooms there.

"Abuelita can teach her much," continued my aunt. *(Snort-snort.)*

"*Sí,*" said *mi ama*.

"Abuelita can heal her before the devil takes her soul." *(Snort-snort-snort.)*

"*Sí,*" said *mi ama*.

"Abuelita can . . ."

"*Voy a la tienda,*" interrupted my drunkle, telling us he was going to go to the store. His words immediately got Tía Luna off my back. "I need some things," he said.

We all looked up. Everyone knew my drunkle wasn't going to the market; he was ditching his own party. After all, this fiesta was lame and it was his fortieth birthday. Surely that would be good for a few tequila shots from a couple of *hombres* at the local bar, wouldn't it?

"*Voy a regresar en diez minutos,*" he said, promising he'd be back in ten minutes. My drunkle grabbed his coat and headed for the door. I found it amazing the way he could lie to a person straight to their face without a hint of care whatsoever.

Tía Luna didn't know what to do or say, so she started snorting tamales at a faster and faster pace. Maybe we would go through all the food after all?

A minute later Papi saved the day.

"Ernesto," said my father just as my drunkle was about to leave. "Now that you are forty, do you think you are man enough for the *habaneros*?"

My drunkle stopped. Slowly, he turned.

"*¿Habaneros?*"

Whenever Mexican men get together, there is

88

always a show to see who was most macho. Often it's tequila. Sometimes it's rooster fights. At my drunkle's fortieth, *mi papi* had just proposed a contest to see who could eat the hottest chile pepper. It was a direct challenge to my drunkle's manhood, and in the world of *machistas*, a direct challenge to someone's manhood could never go unaccepted.

"Alfredo, don't make me laugh. When it comes to habaneros, I will beat you like a lazy mule." My drunkle laughed.

My father took a step toward the patio table in the backyard.

"Sonia," said *mi papi*. "Please, get my chiles."

"*Sí, Papi,*" I said with a smile.

My father took a seat and pulled his chair forward.

"We'll see, Ernesto. We'll see," said *mi papi*. "That is, when you get back from the store."

Mi papi stared at my drunkle, squinting his eyes. My drunkle rubbed his unshaven chin and squinted back. After a moment of intense squinting between the two of them, my drunkle began taking off his coat.

"The store can wait," said my drunkle. "First, the chiles."

It was only the second time I ever remember that

mi papi had gotten the person who worked the Sunday night shift at the gym to cover his Saturday night shift so that he could do something other than be a janitor, but I guess sometimes things just work out in life. And though *mi papi* was no *machista*, when he saw that no one was enjoying the food, no one was dancing, and pretty much no one had even bothered to show up, he knew he had to do something to keep the evening from turning into a complete disaster. A *habanero* contest was the only solution.

And it would be perfect.

My drunkle took a seat across the table from *mi papi*. The few guests who had bothered to come gathered around to watch.

"Me too," said Rodrigo, jumping into a third chair.

My drunkle looked at Rodrigo, and his lips curled to a frown. "This is only for real men, pisshead. Get lost."

Rodrigo's face turned serious. He leaned in close so he was almost nose to nose with my drunkle. "Maybe I'll buy you a bra for your tits now that this birthday has turned you into an old woman," he answered.

Everyone laughed. Part of the fun of *habanero*

contests was all the insults that flew back and forth.

"Can you believe the *vieja* fears me?" Rodrigo added with a giant grin.

My drunkle leaned over, grabbed Rodrigo by his shirt, and issued my brother a serious warning.

"Okay, shit ears, you wanna play? But be warned, because I'm gonna burn a new ring through your asshole," said my drunkle.

"And then my butt will match your face," said Rodrigo. Everyone laughed again.

"Keep clowning, barf chin, keep clowning. But this old man knows a few tricks . . . and you should know, I play dirty."

"Bring it on, *vieja*," said Rodrigo. "Bring it on. I'm right here."

"*Aquí tienes los chiles, Papi,*" I said.

It got quiet as *mi papi* unwrapped a big plastic bag that held an assortment of my father's peppers.

"I want to play too," my eight-year-old brother, Miguel, said, suddenly squirming up to the table.

"Miguelito, no," said *mi ama*. "This is not a thing for you."

"*Sí,*" said Miguel, pulling away from her grip. *Mi ama* tried to grab him, but he yanked his arm away like a spoiled brat.

"Miguel, listen to your mother," said *mi papi*.

"No," answered Miguel.

Everyone stopped and turned to stare at my brother.

"I want to play," he said with a pouty look on his face.

Everyone then looked at my father to see how he would handle his son's tremendous disrespect. Would *mi papi* scream? Would *mi papi* spank him? Would *mi papi* use his belt? In *mi cultura*, children never spoke to their fathers as if they were *pendejos*.

Miguel crossed his arms in disobedience. Of course, all the attention only made my younger brother feel even more powerful. Papi, much to everyone's surprise, allowed his behavior to pass.

"Are you sure you want to play?" my father asked.

"*Sí,*" said Miguel, as stubborn as a mule.

"Okay, have a seat," said *mi papi*, looking over at empty chair number four at the table.

Miguel smiled from ear to ear and jumped into the chair, doing his best to look like a real man. *Mi ama* lowered her eyes. She knew her son was about to experience the wisdom of *mi papi*. And she knew it would be painful.

"So, it's me versus the Rodriguez men," said my drunkle, looking around at his competition. "It makes me laugh that this is the best you have to offer."

My father, paying no attention to the taunts of my drunkle, turned to Miguel. "You pick which chile everyone eats first. Youngest always chooses." Miguel looked at all the choices on the table and studied the peppers. There were two colors of peppers in front of him, red and green. Figuring that the reds were hottest, Miguel chose red for my father, red for my drunkle, and red for Rodrigo. Also figuring the bigger the pepper, the hotter the pepper, Miguel chose for each of his competitors the largest peppers in the batch.

And for himself, Miguel chose a small, green *habanero*. Rodrigo and my drunkle did their best to suppress their laughter.

"Are you sure, *mijo*?" asked *mi papi*. I could only shake my head. Miguel was wrong on both sides. Green peppers were almost always hotter than red peppers, and the smaller the chile, the more heat it usually had. Miguel had pretty much chosen for himself a stick of dynamite.

"*Sí, estoy seguro,*" said Miguel, puffing out his chest. "And don't try to trick me. Eat!" he ordered.

Mi papi, not wanting to be disagreeable, raised the pepper Miguel had chosen for him to his mouth. "Okay, if the man of the house says eat, I guess I must eat."

Miguel smiled. *Mi papi* ate the whole pepper in three chomps. Miguel seemed impressed. Then my drunkle then did the same, except before he put the pepper in his mouth, he called Miguel penis face. Finally Rodrigo ate his. Not one of them blinked from the heat.

Miguel, approving of how well each of the men had handled the hotness of their peppers, figured he too was in for a breeze of a time. He lifted his *habanero*.

"Here," *mi papi* said, interrupting, "let me cut that for you. A small pepper like this can get stuck in your throat or something."

My father took the small green pepper from his son's hands and sliced it into thirds on a plate. Then he began to cut at it a little more. Miguel rudely reached across the table.

"Stop messin' with my chile," said Miguel to our father as he took back his pepper.

What Papi was really trying to do was quickly take some of the seeds and veins out, because that's what gives *habaneros* their heat. But Miguel wanted his pepper back, so my father gave it to him.

"Okay," said *mi papi*, doing as he was told. "Here you go."

My father passed the sliced pieces back to Miguel.

Of course, I was hoping *mi papi*'s quick effort to reduce the chile's heat would help.

It didn't.

About three seconds after the small tip of the green *habanero* entered Miguel's mouth, he began to chew. His teeth were the fuse that lit the dynamite. Flames began to burn, and my brother immediately started to spit. But spitting never works with authentic *habaneros*. Screaming and crying came next, but what did a *habanero* pepper care if my brother screamed and cried? Legend says that authentic *habaneros* have minds of their own, and once they are in your mouth, they dance around like crazy gypsies setting fire to anything they touch. Miguel started to run. His tongue was blazing, tears poured from his eyes, and he yelped in pain. Everyone except *mi ama* laughed.

Trying to get Miguel to calm down, Ama ran to my younger brother and hugged him, but the burn was so intense that he broke away from her grip and raced to the garden hose. We all watched with great amusement as Miguel cranked the hose to full volume and tried to rinse out his mouth with water. However, his lips were burning so badly that no matter how much water Miguel shot down his throat, the flames wouldn't stop. Finally in desperation, Miguel grabbed a handful of dirt and began rubbing it on his tongue. I guess he figured the wet black soil would help stop the pain. After all, when you are *"enchilada,"* as my people like to say, logic abandons you.

People in the yard shrieked with laughter as Miguel ate grass like a cow. After a moment of chomping on earth, Miguel looked over at the people falling all over themselves laughing at him and ran inside the house, embarrassed and ashamed. Everyone in the backyard continued to hoot and roar. It would be half an hour before Miguel would show his face again, and I was sure that for the rest of his life, our family would often retell the story about the time Miguel had turned into the mud-eating pepper boy.

"A lesson earned is a lesson learned," said my father as everything finally settled back down. Then he looked at my drunkle. "Shall we continue?"

"I hope you were paying attention," said my drunkle to Papi. "Because soon it will be like father, like son."

"I pick," said Rodrigo, eager to get on with the fun. My father pushed the bag of chiles in Rodrigo's direction. The contest continued.

Instead of choosing a pepper, however, Rodrigo stood up, went to the cooler, and grabbed himself a beer. It was the first time he'd ever done such a thing in front of my father.

Psst! he opened it and took a sip. But Papi didn't say anything, he just stared. At seventeen years old, *mi hermano* was a boy who thought he was a man.

Rodrigo, acting as if there was nothing odd about his actions, sat back down, took another sip of *cerveza*, and looked through his *habanero* choices. A minute later he had selected peppers for his opponents. Rodrigo wouldn't make the same mistake as Miguelito, he was too old for that. The contest began for real.

I had to admit Rodrigo did better than I thought he would, but chiles are something that take years to develop an *estómago* for, and during round number four, Rodrigo met the pepper that would remove him from the contest.

Within seconds of his first bite, his eyes turned to teardrops. Moments later he looked up with deep concern on his face and told my father, "I can't feel my tongue."

"Finish your pepper," said my drunkle.

Rodrigo wiped the water from his eyes with his sleeves. He raised the second half of the chile to his lips, then paused again.

"The roof of my mouth feels like paint that is peeling."

"Finish or quit," answered my drunkle.

Rodrigo moved the small piece of green fire even

closer to his mouth. His eyes filled with more and more water. The hotter the pepper, the more your eyes tear up.

"My chin is numb."

"Eat."

"Are my lips still on my face?"

"Quit stalling, ass eyes. Eat."

My brother hesitated, already knowing that his insides would burn for a week. Again, Rodrigo wiped his eyes with his sleeve.

"EAT IT!" shouted my drunkle. My brother pushed the pepper to the edge of his teeth . . . and then set the unfinished piece down.

"*No puedo*," he said in defeat. "*Me rindo.*"

And that's when Rodrigo made his real mistake. With his eyes watering so badly, he forgot the golden rule of pepper eating and rubbed the water from his eyes with his fingers instead of his sleeve. Mouths were, of course, somewhat able to handle the heat of *habanero* juice. But a person's eyes, no way.

"Ayyyyy, I'm BLIND!" Rodrigo shouted as he leaped up from the table.

My drunkle immediately tried to help.

"Wait, *cabrón*, listen to me, listen to me! Try rubbing your eyes with your elbows. It's the only thing that will work."

Rodrigo, desperate for relief, paused and did his best to listen to the wisdom of the elders in this most desperate and painful of situations. Taking my drunkle's advice, my brother began to raise his elbows to his eyes.

But of course, a person's elbows cannot reach their eyes. My drunkle began to laugh.

"Raise them higher, pussy nose. Raise them higher!"

At this point, Rodrigo's brain stopped working. Goodness knows why, but he started to run away as fast as he could. It was the first time I had ever seen a person crash into a fence at full speed. Rodrigo bounced off, fell to the ground, and rolled around, grabbing his balls. I guess he must have somehow banged them on the low part of the post. *Mi ama*, thinking quickly, grabbed the garden hose Miguelito had used to stop the fire in his mouth and began to spray Rodrigo. I don't think anyone knew why my mother was spraying the back of his T-shirt with hose water, but she must have figured any kind of wetness was sure to help.

Rodrigo had no idea what was happening, so he tried to stand up and run once again. This time he crashed over a chair and landed face-first in the bushes.

"Use you elbows, ball breath!" shouted my drunkle. "Use your elbows."

Mi ama, desperate to help, stretched out the hose to its full length and stood three feet away from Rodrigo, spraying his pants. From his upside-down position, lying face-first in the bushes, my brother continued to scream. Even Miguel came outside to laugh.

"Two down, one to go," said my drunkle as the commotion with Rodrigo settled. "You dare to continue, Alfredo?"

It took my father a moment to respond, but he didn't do it with speech. Instead he reached across the table, picked up the second half of Rodrigo's half-eaten chile bomb, and plopped it in his mouth.

"Kind of sweet," he said after a few chews. "Good with *carne asada*."

My drunkle and my father exchanged another long squint. A moment later, my drunkle rose to his feet.

"I must piss," he said.

Mi papi nodded and sorted through the remaining peppers. There were about eleven or so various shapes, shades, and sizes. He picked one up and took a nibble just for pleasure.

"Take your time," *mi papi* answered. "I'll be here."

My drunkle disappeared into the house. It was a while before he returned, but when he did, my drunkle had two fresh beers with him, both of them opened. I thought having two open beers at once was kind of weird, but my drunkle did a lot weird things when it came to alcohol, so I let it slide. However, we were sitting next to a cooler filled with *cerveza,* so why had my drunkle gone to the kitchen to get beer? I guess *mi papi*'s reputation for eating peppers caused him to want to be well prepared with liquids for the upcoming battle.

My drunkle took a big sip and sat back down.

"Okay, let's finally see what's in your pants," said my drunkle to my father.

"Same as yours, Ernesto," answered *mi papi.* "Same as yours. Only bigger."

Everyone laughed. The crowd closed in tighter. It was now time for the real heat.

My drunkle and *mi papi* went back and forth and back and forth eating peppers. Truly, it was impressive. Each of them ate chiles that would send the stomach of most billy goats to the hospital. And *mi papi* did it without liquid. He drank nothing. All he did was nibble on a few corn tortillas between bites. My drunkle, of course, slurped beers, but he would have been doing that anyway, contest or not. The two of them ate until every pepper was gone.

"A stalemate," said my drunkle, ready to call it a night and head to the bars.

"*Espera*," said *mi papi*. "Not so fast. Sonia," said *mi papi*, turning to me, "please, go get my box."

"Your box?" I said in disbelief.

"*Sí*, my box," answered Papi.

Mi papi's box was where my father kept his private chile peppers, his secret stash that was too dangerous to leave lying around. In fact, that's why they were in a box, because if he had used only bags to store then, the *habaneros* would have burned a hole right through the plastic.

"What's this about a box?" asked my drunkle with a hint of concern in his voice.

"Yes, and my gloves," my father instructed, not answering the question. It wasn't even wise to touch these peppers with bare hands.

A look of worry flashed across the eyes of my drunkle. I went to the garage where *mi papi* kept his stash. Two minutes later I returned with my father's private box of *habanero* peppers.

"*Estos son los chiltepins, la madre de todos los chiles*," my father explained as he spread out the legendary chiles. They were chiltepins, the mother of all peppers. "But you don't have to continue if you don't want, Ernesto. After all, I'd hate to ruin your birthday," my father said.

"My birthday present will be setting your insides on fire," my drunkle replied, though clearly worried about the chiltepins.

My father slid the garden glove over his fingers and reached into the box. My drunkle put on the other glove from the pair I had brought. The two of them looked like Mexican Michael Jacksons.

"Let's hope these have a bit of heat, huh?" said my drunkle in an effort to sound bold and unafraid. Then he took another big gulp of beer, finishing what was left in the first bottle. A second later, he took a gulp from beer number two. The challenge was on.

Using a garden glove, my drunkle picked up a nasty-looking little chile for my father to eat. It was the first pepper we had seen with a streak of yellow in it.

My drunkle passed the pepper to *mi papi*. It was less than an inch long. My father didn't even hesitate. Using his gloved hand to hold the pepper, he grabbed the *habanero*, bit the whole thing down to the stem, and started to chew. All was quiet beneath his furry mustache. Everyone stared.

Unlike with the earlier peppers, this time it was a slow, deliberate chew *mi papi* used. And many tears

came to his eyes. We all watched in silence as he con-
centrated deeply. It was as if he were inhaling and
exhaling with that special type of rhythmic breathing
pregnant women used during childbirth.

After about ninety seconds, *mi papi* finally swallowed. Another minute passed before he spoke.

"A touch of kick," he said as he tore off a small
piece of tortilla and started to nibble on it. "Yes . . .
some kick," he repeated softly.

I looked at *mi papi*. The pupils of his eyes were
dilated as big as coins. Next it was my drunkle's turn.

Mi papi reached into the metal box and pulled out
a chile for my drunkle, a medium-size reddish-orange
habanero. One look at it would not have indicated to
anyone but the most knowledgeable of pepper people
that *mi papi* had just selected a nuclear warhead.

Using the gardener's glove, he passed it to my
drunkle. My drunkle took his time and studied the
pepper.

"Where are these from again?" asked my drunkle,
curious to know about the origin of *mi papi's* secret
stash.

"Xalapa," he answered.

"Xalapa?" replied my drunkle, a bit taken aback.
Xalapa was infamous for its chile peppers. People
said the region marked the doorway to hell because

no one other than Satan could eat such hot *habaneros*.

"You can still quit," offered *mi papi*.

My drunkle stared him in the eyes and squinted. Everyone knew he wanted to quit. Everyone knew it made sense to quit. Everyone knew he should quit.

But his pride got in the way.

"Never," said my drunkle. "In two more minutes, I'm going to melt the teeth out of your mouth."

At the time, none of us had any idea that my drunkle had been cheating all along. It turned out those weren't beers he was drinking; they were beer bottles filled with olive oil. My dirtbag drunkle had filled up two empty *cervezas* with olive oil from the kitchen so that he could coat his tongue and protect his mouth from the heat of the peppers. It was an old Navajo Indian trick; but when he ate the *habaneros de Xalapa*, his cheating plan backfired.

My drunkle took a bite and slowly started to chew. A moment later, he curled over and fell to the ground as if he had been shot in the stomach with a cannon.

Greenish liquid started to ooze from his lips. Tía Luna cried out, "Call an ambulance!" but there would be no stopping the volcano. Hot lava began shooting out of both ends of my drunkle's body. He quickly stood and vomited his way to the bathroom, holding his rear end like a four-year-old who had to poop but wasn't going to make it to the toilet in time. Aside from the fact that it was outrageously disgusting and my aunt was genuinely fearful for my drunkle's life, I laughed and laughed and laughed as if it were the funniest thing I had ever seen.

And that's when I realized I had been totally wrong about this birthday party. It was the best fiesta I'd ever been to.

Tía Luna scowled at me.

For the next three hours my drunkle stayed locked in the bathroom, moaning and groaning and vomiting and diarrheaing. I imagined sometimes he sat on the toilet, other times he kneeled in front of the toilet— and back and forth and back and forth. The *habaneros de Xalapa* had proven to be too much for him, a quart of oil in his system or not.

Mi papi put the garden glove back on his hand and tossed the rest of the peppers into the box.

"Throw those away," ordered *mi ama*. "You'll kill somebody."

"Bahh, these peppers aren't for eating," my father answered. "*Habaneros de Xalapa* are my secret ingredient for removing rust off the garden tools. Why do you think I keep them in the garage?"

I smiled ear to ear.

"Sonia," said *mi papi*, handing me the box. "Please, put these back."

"*Sí, Papi,*" I answered, heading gleefully to the garage.

Tía Luna turned to *mi ama*. "Do you see how she takes pleasure in other people's pain?" she said.

Mi ama nodded.

"She needs Abuelita," said my aunt, plowing a bite of birthday cake into her mouth.

Mi ama nodded again.

I headed to the garage, not really trying to hide my happiness. For the rest of the evening, every time my uncle farted, he moaned.

And I smiled.

chapter trece

We had so much extra food on Sunday that my aunt invited her church group over for a lunch buffet. Church ladies, I'd discovered, could always be counted on for two things: damning sinners and accepting free food. Our house was packed with disciples of the Savior who had appetites the size of sumo wrestlers.

They ate everything in sight, making a ton of crumbs, spilling salsa, and leaving half-empty soda cups everywhere as they did it. Plus, every time someone took a tamale, Tía Luna told them not to expect much because they'd been made by a girl with *manos poseídas por el Diablo*, hands possessed by the devil. The women would stare at me, frown, then munch away like porky pigs in a barn anyway.

When my drunkle woke up at two o'clock in the afternoon and stumbled into the living room, he found himself surrounded by a bunch of Jesus ladies wearing big hats, his butt hole burning like lava rocks. I'm sure he thought he had died and gone to hell. At least he sure looked like he had.

But Tía Luna looked happy. Maybe my drunkle's fortieth birthday party had been a bust, but the Church Brunch Tamale Buffet was a grand-slam success. (Praise Jesus!) Those ladies ate and yapped and crossed themselves until almost nine o'clock that night. By the time they left, our house looked as if a hurricane had blown through. Of course I was the one who had to clean it up. I missed a fourth day of school.

That afternoon, I had a surprise visitor.

"Yo, girl, I thought you evaporated off the planet."

It was Tee-Ay.

"No, I just have some stuff to do around here," I responded, happy to see her. I took her into the living room.

"My uncle's back," I told her in a soft voice.

"Again?" she said.

"Uh-huh."

Even though he had actually been back for a while, I somehow hadn't gotten around to informing Tee about it yet.

"Why doesn't your dad give him the boot?" Tee-Ay asked.

"He's my mom's brother."

She rolled her eyes.

"What can I say?" I added. "He's family."

"So," she said.

"*Tú no entiendes a la familia,*" I answered. "We do things differently."

In *mi cultura*, we always put family first. Always. It's what makes us strong. We support one another. We sacrifice for one another. We do what we can to be there for one another—even for those who are struggling. No, my people may not have a lot of money, but we do have values. More than lots of other kinds of Americans do, at least. (Though I wouldn't dare mention that to Tee-Ay. That could set off a nuclear war.)

"What about doing for you?" she asked me.

"We do for each other," I answered.

"How's that fair?"

"I told you, Tee. It's family."

Suddenly, my drunkle stumbled in. He rubbed his hands through his greasy hair then looked at Tee-Ay as if she were nothing more than a cockroach.

"*Oye, Sonia. ¿Qué pasa?*" he asked.

"*Nada,*" I answered. "*Todo está bien, Tío.*"

110

My drunkle paused, scratched his chin, turned, and wandered into the bathroom. A moment later, we heard a loud fart.

"That just ain't right," Tee-Ay said, shaking her head in disapproval. "You gotta represent for yourself, girl."

"You just don't get it, Tee. You just don't get it."

Though we went to the same school, took the same classes, drank from the same bottles of Diet Pepsi, and shared the same french fries, there were a million miles separating me and Tee. Funny how just a little bit of darker skin pigmentation can change so much between two people.

"You know what, Sonia?" Tee-Ay said, getting ready to rip in to me.

I looked up. *What?* I thought.

There was a pause.

"Aw, I'm just gonna bounce," she said, stopping herself mid-sentence before she spoke some words I'm sure we both would have regretted. Tee-Ay bent down and grabbed her backpack.

"But you just got here," I said, not wanting her to leave.

"Yeah, I should go. I only stopped by to bring you some schoolwork so you wouldn't get left too far behind." She reached into her bag and tossed some papers onto the table. I glanced at them, then laughed.

"What?" she snapped. "You screwing up in school ain't funny, Sonia. It ain't funny at all." Wow, was she mad.

But Tee-Ay didn't understand. I wasn't laughing at the schoolwork. I was laughing at the fact that I had already done it. All of it. And more. Over the past few nights I had already guessed where my teachers would be going in class and worked ahead so that I could keep up my grades.

"I already did it," I said, looking at the papers. "Yeah. Tomorrow's too."

Tee-Ay paused while she pieced it all together.

"What a dork!" she finally said with a grin.

"Wanna share some *papas*?" I asked. "I'm kinda hungry."

"Absolutely," Tee-Ay said, putting her backpack down. A minute later we were in the kitchen where I cooked us up some sliced potatoes, nice and crispy with salt and ketchup. I even had a Diet Pepsi in the fridge we were able to share. For the next fifteen minutes we laughed and ate and just did a whole lot of talking about a whole lot of nothing, exactly like we would have done at school. It felt good.

Then my drunkle walked in, drawn like a wild animal by the smell of food.

"*Sonia,*" he said, sniffing the air. "*Tengo hambre. ¿Qué tenemos?*"

I looked at Tee-Ay and lowered my eyes. Break time was over.

"*Puedo hacer huevos y papas con salsa ranchera si tú quieres, Tío,*" I said softly, offering to cook him up a Mexican omelet.

He paused to think about whether it was good enough.

"*Está bien,*" he answered. "*Pero apúrate. Tengo hambre,*" he added, telling me to hurry up. Then he exited the kitchen, expecting me to call him when his food was ready.

Tee-Ay picked up her things and prepared to leave, but I wanted her to stay. There was so much more to tell her; about Geraldo, about Tía Luna, the things that had been going on with my drunkle.

"Good to see you," Tee-Ay said as she headed for the door. "And get back to school."

I paused before answering. Inside my head a voice screamed, *Please don't go. Don't Go!*

"I will," I answered as I forced a smile. Tee-Ay reached for the door handle.

Don't go! the voice screamed again. *Please, Tee-Ay, don't go!*

"Thanks for stopping by," I added.

We hugged. I felt my stomach gurgle. Tee-Ay left.

"*Sonia . . .*" called a voice from the other room. "*¿Qué pasa? Te dije que tengo hambre.*"

I headed to the kitchen, took some eggs out of the refrigerator, and decided that no matter what, I was going to go to school the next day. I didn't care what anyone said. We could throw a party for Jesus himself, I was NOT making any more tamales.

And if Jesus did come, he'd better bring some apostles to clean up the mess, because I was through.

I was completely and totally through.

chapter catorce

I returned to school the next day, expecting to get into a little bit of trouble for missing so much class, but hardly a teacher said squat to me about having been absent for four days in a row. They didn't ask where I'd been. They didn't ask for a note. They didn't ask for any assignments. I just turned them in on my own. It was as if no one even cared if I came to high school. I guess in their eyes, I was just another *Mexicanita*, here today, gone tomorrow, with many, many more to follow.

Actually, one teacher did say something to me, my World History teacher, Mr. Wardin. It was after I handed him the homework for the days I'd been out.

"Well, Ms. Rodríguez," he said in his intellectual voice. "With such an atrocious attendance record, I would not have expected the shrewd decision to keep up with your studies the way you have. It's almost oxymoronic." He paused. "Do you know what the word *oxymoronic* means, Ms. Rodríguez?"

I lowered my eyes.

"Just try coming to class more a bit more frequently than you cruise the shopping mall, Ms. Rodríguez. In case you didn't know it, in this country, your education matters greatly."

When school was over that day I wasn't sure what had me feeling worse, the fact that no one seemed to care or the thought that the one person at school who did care had made me feel like an ignorant wetback. Either way, I was bummed out and needed a pick-me-up.

But unfortunately, Frijolito was gone.

I stared in Santiago's front window for five minutes, watching a group of new kittens wrestle and play and body slam each other. The new cats were all cute and fluffy and happy.

I hated them all.

Maybe Frijolito had been moved somewhere else, I thought. I went inside. The bell on the door jingled as I entered.

"*¡Hola! ¡Hola!*" said a parakeet when I walked in.

"*Cállate,*" I said to the dumb bird as I closed the door behind me. "This is America; speak English."

I looked around, but Frijolito wasn't nowhere. I hoped he had gone to a good home. One without a drunkle.

The pet shop boy with the emerald green eyes, Geraldo wasn't around either, but it had been a long time since I'd seen him, so who knew what could have happened? Maybe he'd found a new job. Maybe he'd found a new place to live. Maybe he'd found a new girl.

Maybe it was a white girl.

I hope she chokes on a grape, I thought as I turned to leave. White girls always ate grapes.

"You would like to hold him?" came a voice. I smiled. But I smiled on the inside because I didn't want the stupid rude boy to see me.

"*Free-ho-lee-toe!*" I said as I turned around and took the cat in my arms. Wow, my little bean had grown bigger. And more cute, too.

"You thought he was sold, didn't you?"

"No," I answered, not wanting to give Geraldo the satisfaction of being right.

"Oh, I know you did," he replied. "But what kind of customer is going to buy a lopsided cat?"

"He's not lopsided," I snapped back. "He's just . . . unique, that's all." I stroked Frijolito's fur. He purred.

"*Sí*, he's very 'unique.' This is why I've been

117

keeping him in the back, so no one else decides to buy this 'unique' creature."

"In the back all by himself?" I said, concerned that little Frijolito was not getting proper care and attention.

"*Relájate,*" answered Geraldo. "He gets nothing but VIP treatment. Special food, all the best toys, and lots of space to play."

I smiled.

"Being that he's already in your heart, I am hoping maybe he'll show me the path."

Geraldo's eyes twinkled. I felt my face go flush.

"I missed you, Sonia," he said. "I missed you very much. Must you make me wait so long to see you?"

"We cannot 'see' each other," I said.

"Of course we can. And we will. Remember, it is written."

"I remember nothing."

"You remember Snickers bars and vegetable soup, I bet. Come," he said, and led me to the back of the store, past the sign that said EMPLOYEES ONLY, and into the storage room. At first I didn't want to go, but of course I was curious about what he wanted to show me, so I followed behind. And then, on a table filled with rabbit food and fish-tank water supplies, I saw a small, cleared-out space with an elegant dinner setting. There was a white plate, a cloth napkin, and a silver fork, spoon, and knife.

And in the center of the plate was a brand-new, not-yet-unwrapped Snickers bar alongside a can of vegetable soup.

"Are you ready for our first date?" asked Geraldo as he lit a small candle he had set up next to the water glass.

I didn't know what to say. Obviously, Geraldo had been planning this moment for a long time. Truly, I couldn't believe he had done all this for me. I just stared.

"Your sadness has such beauty, Sonia, but you carry too much of it. Your heart needs to smile," he said. "A *corazón* without laughter is a *corazón* that will not survive."

Geraldo smiled and my heart melted, so much so that I almost began to cry inside the stupid pet store. Geraldo was the kindest, most thoughtful boy I had ever met.

I looked deeply into his eyes and lost myself. I had never wanted to kiss a boy so badly in all my life. Frijolito purred.

"We can't," I said, suddenly breaking off my gaze.

"But we will," he answered.

"I must go," I said, turning for the door.

"Give me your phone number," he said.

"No."

"Yes."

"No."

"Here is paper. Please, write it down."

He passed me the paper and a pen.

"I can't," I told him. Then I wrote down my phone number.

"Here. And take the cat before I rip my number up," I said, passing him Frijolito.

"Go ahead," he answered. "Tear it up, if that's what you really want."

I paused.

"Okay, I'll do it for you," he said, and then sure enough, Geraldo tore the piece of paper with my phone number on it into a thousand little pieces and tossed them into the air like confetti. I looked at him like he was crazy, completely not understanding why he had just done what he did.

"I memorized it the moment the pen touched the paper." he said with a smile. "It is etched like stone into my brain."

I lowered my eyes and left. I want to say that I wish I hadn't given him my number, but I was glad I did. And I want to say that I was hoping that he wouldn't call, but I was hoping he would. Geraldo didn't seem like other boys. He was so nice, so gentle-manlike, so confident and handsome.

Maybe Geraldo really was different from other boys.

Then again, didn't all other boys seem different from all other boys? I mean, that's probably what Constancy had thought about Rickee before she got pregnant at the age of sixteen.

It was so obvious when I saw Constancy at school during lunch a few weeks later. The baggy clothes, the look of always being tired. I had never been really close with her the way I was with Tee-Ay (after all, I never even called Constancy "Cee-Saw," like her other friends did), but when I saw her turn Kermit-the-Frog green at the sight of a simple french fry, I knew something had to be up. Besides, seeing a teenage girl trying to hide her pregnancy, well, it feels like I've grown up around that stuff my whole life.

One afternoon I decided to help. After all, helping others seemed to be one of the only things I was any good at. Besides, if I was in Constancy's situation, I'd certainly hope someone would help me, so on my way home from *escuela*, I purchased some ginger candy and saltine crackers (the real kind, not the fake ones). Then, when I got home, I put my things down on the dining room table to go into the kitchen. When I came back into the room, I found Tía Luna with her nose all up in my business. She held up the saltines.

"¿*Qué es eso?*" she asked.

"*Nada,*" I answered.

"Fornicator!" she shouted.

"It's not for me," I replied.

"*¡Mentirosa!*" she yelled back, calling me a liar. "It's the work of *el Diablo.*" She gave me a slow, evil eye and then headed into *mi ama*'s bedroom.

Let her believe what she wants, I thought as I packed the things back into a brown paper bag. I know the real truth.

When I handed Constancy the bag the next day at school, she glared at Tee-Ay with a laser beam look that could have burned a hole through a steel door.

"What? I didn't say nothin'!" Tee-Ay said in her own defense.

A minute later, after I explained to Constancy how she should stay away from spicy foods and how what I had given her would help with the nausea, she started crying on my shoulder. I have to admit, it was kind of weird to be hugging someone I didn't really feel that close to, but I hugged Constancy anyway and told her that it would be all right.

That's when I realized my aunt was right. I was a *mentirosa.* I was a liar because, in my heart, I didn't

122

think it was going to be all right. I didn't think it was going to be all right at all.

Constancy had no job, no education, and no man in her life who would step up and help her raise this baby. For a sixteen-year-old minority girl with a bun in her oven—no, I didn't think it was going to be all right at all.

But still, that's what I told her. Really, what else was I supposed to say?

"Ssshh, it'll be okay," I said as she wept on my shoulder. "Ssshh."

Yep, I thought. Just another mess left by yet another *Príncipe* Charming from the hood. *Qué sorpresa*.

That night Geraldo called three times. I didn't speak to him once. Instead, I did my homework. And an extra credit assignment for World History class.

Men are pigs.

chapter quince

"Pero no quiero," I said a month later.

"Sonia, ya es bastante. Tú vas," mi ama answered.
"Sólo y Rodrigo."

But I didn't want to go to Mexico. And I most certainly didn't want to go with just Rodrigo in just two days.

"Pero, Ama . . ." I said, hoping that whining would help.

It didn't.

"¡Finalmente!" she said. *"Tú vas a México."* And that was the end of that. *Mi ama* returned to her room and closed the door. A minute later, the television went on.

When I was a kid, our whole *familia* would go to Mexico for the summer. Back then it was easy for people to just cross and recross the border, but now the borders have tightened, and my parents, since they don't have papers, can't risk not being able to reenter the United States. That's why, like most illegals, now that they are here, they stay. We need the money.

The truth is, people mostly only come to the United States for the dollar bills. In Mexico, many workers make about two dollars a day, but in El Norte they can make twelve to fifteen dollars an hour for doing the same job. I mean, America thinks it's so great, but not every person who comes here wants to stay forever. A lot of people just want to make cash and go back to their families but now that the borders are way stricter, it's too dangerous to do that. And to sneak into the United States nowadays means you have to take life-threatening risks. Four-year-olds walk in 110-degree heat with no *agua*. Pregnant women swim through polluted rivers. People die on their way to this country. Many people die. They die for a chance at opportunity, an opportunity that I already have.

And now *mi ama* was sending me back? Heck, if Mexico was so great, why did they even come here in the first place?

"You don't know how lucky you are to be able to visit your home," *mi ama* said.

"This is my home," I answered.

"This is not a home," she said. "This is El Norte."

I hated the way *mi ama* always acted as if one day we were going to leave. We were never leaving. We are Mexicans who have become Americans, and we are here to stay, even if my parents don't have any papers. After all these years, I just didn't understand why she still didn't get that.

Besides, I didn't want to go anywhere else. This country may not be her home, but it certainly is mine.

Isn't it?

"Here are your tickets," *mi ama* said, handing me an envelope she pulled from her dresser drawer. "I got a good price on them."

I looked at the airline reservations.

"But this leaves in two days! Eight days before school is out," I said.

"I saved twenty percent," *mi ama* answered.

"What about *mi escuela*?" I asked.

"Tell your teachers you are leaving early."

"They don't just let you leave early."

"Enough!" my mother shouted. "Who is in charge around here, anyway? Who knows what's best for you?"

I didn't answer the question, but I sure didn't think it was her. The next day at school was horrible.

"No."

"No?" I repeated with an uncertain look.

He paused and glared.

"No," he said a second time. "Okay, wait," he said. "How about this? What if I just let everyone leave eight days early?" he replied in a sarcastic voice. "Hey, class," Mr. Wardin called to the entire room. "Good news: we're going to let you out of school two weeks early because Ms. Rodríguez is heading to a beach in Mexico and needs to get her lounge chair set up before the rest of the vacationers get all the good spots by the water."

The other students hardly even looked up from their World History work. They knew Mr. Wardin was just being a jerk.

"Or better yet, Ms. Rodriguez," he said, turning back to me. "Why don't we just cancel final exams altogether? After all, an eleven-week summer vacation to smoke weed, have sex, and play video games is hardly enough time at all, now that I think about it." He called out to the class a second time. "Also, class, I've decided school is canceled today, too, because I want to leave early and go eat tacos with my homies."

I looked down. There was no need to embarrass me.

"You do realize, Ms. Rodríguez, that if it were up to me, I'd cancel summer vacation entirely and make kids go to class year round. You people need more school, not less. Tell your mother the answer is no. There is no way to take any of your tests early, and if you miss class, your grade will suffer."

"How much?" I asked in a low voice.

Mr. Wardin rolled his eyes then slowly opened his grade book.

"You know, with as much school as you've already missed, it's pretty incredible that you have managed to maintain a B- so far. But if you leave, your grade will most assuredly drop to a D."

"A D?" I said, thinking about all the hard work I had done this year.

"Be grateful it's not an F, Ms. Rodríguez," he said, closing his grade book. "Besides, who is in charge around here, anyway? I mean, really, who do you think knows what's best for you?"

I didn't answer, but I sure didn't think it was Mr. Wardin.

I went home and tried one last time to talk to my mom, telling her exactly what Mr. Wardin had said about my grades.

"Make sure you pack gifts for your cousins," she responded. "It's rude to show up from El Norte without lots of gifts."

The next day, I would be on a plane.

chapter dieciséis

I was mad. I was mad at my aunt for sticking her nose in my business. I was mad at my teachers for lowering my grades without even giving me a chance to do make-up work. I was mad at my mom for wanting me to one day turn into her. That night I brushed my teeth so hard I almost scrubbed the white off of them.

I didn't want to go to stupid Mexico to learn the "ways of the old world," so I could be brainwashed into having lots of babies and running a household. I was already running a household. I had bigger dreams than that. But of course, because I was a girl, what did it matter what my dreams were?

Why didn't anybody ever take my feelings into consideration?

I was so angry I threw open the bathroom door and crashed right into the chest of my drunkle. I crunched my eyebrows and glared at him. Though I had hardly seen him in three days, I was mad at him too. Even when I was in a good mood, I was always mad at him.

He smiled as if he found my anger funny. At least going away would mean no drunkle for two months. I pushed past him without bothering to say a word. When I walked by, he turned to check out my butt as I jiggled away in my pajamas. I didn't care. All I wanted was make sure I had packed enough tampons. The thought of using cheap Mexican tampons the whole summer sent a chill up my spine.

Maybe that's what I'll bring as a gift for the cousins, I thought as I packed a third box of Playtex into my suitcase. American tampons.

I looked at my plane ticket and wanted to cry, but of course, I held it in. I hated my mom. And obviously, she hated me. There was just one thing left for me to do before I left.

"I know why you're here," he said with a big smile when I showed up the next day. "For a Snickers bar and a cup of vegetable soup."

"Stop calling my house, and go find another girl," I said in the rudest voice I could muster up. "I'm leaving for the summer."

"I'll wait," he answered, not bothered one bit by the news.

"Didn't you hear me? I am being sent to Mexico

for the entire summer, and when I come back, I am still not going to contact you. Find another girl, Geraldo," I said. He stood up from stocking bags of doggie treats on the shelf and headed toward the supply room.

A minute later Geraldo brought out Frijolito. As soon as I took the cat in my arms, he began to purr.

"There is no other girl," Geraldo said as I stroked the cat. "There is only you."

A tear began to fall down my cheek.

"You don't even know me," I said.

"There you are wrong," Geraldo replied. "I feel as if I have always known you. Now I just wish to know you better."

He gently wiped the tear from my cheek. I looked up into his shimmering, green eyes. The color was more deep, more dark and soulful than I had ever seen them.

"Know that I will wait," he said. "For you I will wait a thousand years."

Geraldo leaned in and gave me a kiss on the cheek. It was tender. I passed Frijolito back to him and headed for the door.

"Don't," I said. "Don't waste your time on me, Geraldo. I'm not worth it."

And then I left. For Mexico.

chapter diecisiete

I knew things were going to be different the moment Rodrigo and I got on the plane. Five minutes after takeoff, the stewardess asked us what we wanted to drink. I asked for a Coke. So did Rodrigo.

With rum.

¿Qué? I thought.

I was shocked that he had the nerve to order it. And I was even more shocked that the stewardess brought it for him. Couldn't she see he was totally below legal drinking age?

"One Coke and rum," she said with a smile. "That'll be five dollars."

"*Gracias,*" said Rodrigo, taking the drink. Then he reached into his wallet, a red-and-green one that proudly proclaimed *Hecho en México* on the front, and looked up as if there were a problem. "*Pero,* I only have a hundred," he said, flashing two one hundred dollar bills. Rodrigo made a big show of the money, as if he were some kind of international banker or something.

"*Lo siento*," said the stewardess. "But I can't make change for something that big."

At first, I wasn't sure where Rodrigo had got all that money. A moment later, I figured it out.

Mi ama had given us each two hundred dollars as spending cash for our trip. Me, I had made sure that I went out and got small bills so that I wouldn't have a problem paying for things this summer. I turned the twenties she had given me into lots of ones and fives. Rodrigo had gone out and made change too—except he did the opposite and had obviously turned his twenties into hundreds. Ooh, was he sneaky. With bills so big, practically no one where we were going would be able to make change for him.

And that meant Rodrigo could avoid paying for things.

"*Ningún problema*, beautiful lady," my brother replied. "*Sonia, págale a la mujer. Yo después te pago.*"

Huh? I thought. Why was I the stupid one who had to pay? Like my brother was really going to pay me back.

Both of them stared at me, waiting for some cash. I shook my head, reached into my purse, and gave the stewardess a five-dollar bill. Rodrigo's hand then reached into my wallet and pulled out two additional singles.

"Don't forget to give her a tip, cheapo," he said.

The stewardess smiled at Rodrigo with a sexy look in her eye. "I never heard anybody order it as a Coke and rum before," she commented. "It's kinda cute."

"¿Sí?" answered Rodrigo. "Well, once you get to know me better, you'll see that I do a lot of things that are kinda cute."

He laughed. She laughed. Then they both laughed at the fact that they were both laughing. Was this stewardess flirting with him?

Ugh. I was gonna puke.

"*De nada, señor,*" she said in a sexy voice as she put my tip money into her uniform.

"*Por supuesto,*" Rodrigo answered. The look in his eyes said it all: MILE HIGH CLUB. I looked in the seat pocket in front of me for an air-sickness bag. Vomiting suddenly became a real possibility.

After watching the stewardess wiggle away, Rodrigo turned to me and raised his glass. "To *México!*" he said, clinking plastic cups with me in a toast. As much as I didn't want to go on this trip was as much as he did.

Ten minutes later, Rodrigo ordered another Coke and rum. I paid for the second one too, but this time I didn't give the stewardess a tip.

A half an hour later, Rodrigo ordered a third.

"*¡Escúchame!* I'll jump out of this plane without a parachute before I'll pay for another one of your drinks, *me entiendes*, Rigo?" I said to my brother with a glare. But he was already drunk, so he just laughed at me. To him, the whole summer would be nothing but smiles and alcohol and trying to sex up Mexican girls who he had fooled into thinking he was rich.

When we got off the plane we were picked up by one of Abuelita's neighbors, a ranchero who took us on a three-hour drive to the middle of nowhere. And in Mexico, when they say the middle of nowhere, they really mean the middle of nowhere.

Rodrigo called "Shotgun!" and jumped into the front seat before I even realized there wasn't enough room for us to sit up front, so I was forced to sit in the back next to the luggage, a big tractor tire, and a dog that hadn't been washed since the Mexican Revolutionary war.

"Back there I have to sit?" I said. My biggest

concern about sitting in the back was the wind making a total mess of my hair, because I wanted to look good when I first met Abuelita. After all, I hadn't seen her in years and she was so old that I was sure a few smiles, a few hugs, and a few fake conversations about how I was being a good girl back in the United States would be all I'd need to keep her off my back. No doubt she had heard all sorts of lies about me. A good first impression would be important.

"Sorry, no room up front for three," answered the ranchero as he went to load our bags into the back.

I turned to Rodrigo with eyes that begged him to allow me to trade seats with him. My brother looked at me, smiled, and reached for the door.

So he could lock it.

"Should have been quicker, lame-o."

"But, Rigo, my hair."

"Hey, I got hair too," he said, lifting his baseball cap.

"Thanks," I said, climbing into the back of the truck. The ranchero finished loading our suitcases and then climbed into the driver's seat.

"Aren't you going to let the lady ride in the front?" the ranchero asked my brother. In old-world Mexico, being a proper gentleman was still a big deal.

Rodrigo shrugged his shoulders. "I offered," he

said. "But she told me she prefers to ride in the back." Rodrigo turned to me and smiled. "She likes the wind."

"Oh, *bueno*," said the ranchero, satisfied with my brother's answer. "Well, she'll get plenty of it." A minute later we pulled away.

As we bumped along through the countryside, my rear end bounced up and down on the hard, metal floor as if my butt were made of stainless steel. And wind blew through the truck as if I were in the middle of a hurricane. Stupid Rodrigo, I thought. I tried to sit in a corner where the tornado wasn't so bad, but no matter what I did, it was pretty much no use. I was in the middle of a cyclone.

As we drove along, I noticed hills and trees and *pueblitos*. However, the thing that stuck out the most for me was the litter. Bottles, cans, hamburger wrappers, Styrofoam containers, you name it, lay scattered by the side of the road. Even as we moved farther and farther away from the city, it was still very polluted. Most of the items, I noticed, were American products. Pepsi and Burger King seemed to be the favorites, but there were a lot of beer bottles as well.

About twenty minutes into the trip, I started to hear a strange noise.

Slrrrp! Slrrrp!

What the . . . ? I thought.

At first I thought we were getting a flat tire, but as we drove on I realized the sounds were coming from inside the truck, not outside. I looked around but could not find anything.

Slrrrp! Slrrrp!

Finally the sound was driving me so crazy, I got to my knees so I could figure out where the stupid noise was coming from. Wind and dust screamed through my hair as I sat up in the back of the truck. We hit a bump, and I was nearly tossed overboard, like a person on the rail of a cruise ship.

But what the heck was that strange sound, I kept wondering.

I climbed up a bit higher and peeked behind the tractor tire. That's when I found the source of the noise. The dirty dog was licking his balls.

Slrrrp! Slrrrp!

"Stop that," I said.

Slrrrp! Slrrrp!

"Stop! You're grossing me out."

The dog raised its eyes with a stupid look on its face and paused. He had big, swollen testicles.

"No more," I commanded. "You freak."

The dog lowered its leg and stopped. I sat back down, mad about the fact that my hair had gotten even more messed up, but happy that I had at least put an end to the disgusting sound. After all, we still had another few hours in the back of the truck together.

The bumpy ride continued. Some roads were paved, others were not.

Slrrrp! Slrrrp!

"Stop!" I shouted.

The dog stopped. Minutes later it started again.

We argued back and forth for forty-five minutes. Every time I would climb to my knees and take a face full of dust and wind, the dog would show me his balloon balls then lower his leg and stop licking his crotch. And every time I sat back down and huddled away from the screaming wind, the dog would start to slurp his nuts again. Finally I gave up and realized I had been wrong about Mexico. It wasn't all polluted. How could I even think that when I was sharing the back of a pickup truck with a dog who had the cleanest *huevos* in all of North America?

When we arrived at Abuelita's house I thanked the ranchero for the ride, though I don't know why. The way my butt hurt from all the bouncing on hard metal, being dragged the whole way by my thumbs would have been more comfortable.

"*Gracias, señor.*"

"My pleasure; you were nice guests. Weren't

they nice guests?" the ranchero asked the dog in a silly, singsong voice. "Yes, you're a good boy. Good boy."

The dog started licking the ranchero's face, smothering his owner with doggy kisses.

Ugh.

"Yes, Good boy. Good boy. Do you want to give your new friend a kiss good-bye?" the ranchero asked the mutt.

"Uh, *gracias*," I said quickly, walking away before *Señor Huevos* had a chance to lick me.

After a few more doggie kisses, the ranchero climbed back into his truck, waved good-bye, and drove away. A dust cloud rose from his back tires as he left the property.

Rodrigo turned to me. I expected him to say something like, "Well, we're here," or "Home, sweet home." Instead, with his usual charm, he informed me of something different.

"I gotta dump."

"You're gross," I answered.

"What? All that bouncing around stirred up my stomach."

He thought his ride was bumpy?

"Can't you wait till we say hello to Abuelita?" I said

Rodrigo farted. "Nope." He started to walk away.

"Where are you going?" I asked, noticing that he was walking away from, and not to, the house. "Don't go in the bushes."

"I'm going to the bathroom, dummy," he said as he pointed toward a wooden shed.

Oh no, I said to myself. I totally forgot . . . the outhouse. Abuelita didn't have an indoor bathroom. Rodrigo opened the door to the wooden shed, and a frog the size of a rabbit hopped out.

"Get! Go on, get out of here," he said as he closed the door behind him. "I gotta poop."

Great, I thought as I watched the toad hop away. Wild Country Safari Toilet, just like home.

"Estoy aquí," a voice called out from around the side of the house. *"Ven, ven,"* it instructed. "Come here."

I put my things down and quickly tried to fix my hair, but it was no use, the wind had made me look like a tornado victim. I might as well have stuck my finger in an electrical outlet.

"Around back," called the voice.

"Coming," I said, and turned the corner, pushed my bangs to the left, and got ready to offer up my biggest "Hi there!" smile. Then I froze.

In front of me stood a four-hundred-year-old

woman with skin like a wrinkled alligator. She had one tooth, an index finger that was bent sideways as if permanently dislocated, and boobs that drooped to her knees.

And in her left hand she held a machete that was dripping blood.

"*Bienvenida,*" she said.

Suddenly she grabbed a chicken that was standing next to her, twisted its neck with a loud *crrr-ack*, and *BAM!* chopped off its head.

The chicken went running. Well, at least its body did. Its head just rolled onto the ground with one eye looking out to see what had happened. Blood spurted everywhere.

"*¿Tuvieron un buen viaje?*" the old woman asked me, inquiring if I'd had a good trip.

I stared in horror as the body ran helplessly in circles, searching for a way to reattach its head. Red liquid spouted from the open pipe in its neck while the eye on the ground looked directly at me as if I was the one who had done this to it. Finally, the headless body ran into a fence, bounced off like a pinball, and fell to the ground. Without a brain, it was unable to get up.

But it twitched.

After five or six convulsions, the body died, but I still wasn't sure about the head. Since chickens don't have eyelids, the eyeball just stared and stared and stared at me.

"I hope you're hungry," said my grandmother in Spanish as she picked up the bird by its feet and tossed it onto a pile of dead chickens. "Because tonight," she continued as she started to kick the sliced-off chicken head like a soccer ball into a pile of other sliced-off chicken heads, "we've planned a grand fiesta."

I stood there frozen, as if my feet had been nailed to the ground.

"*Hola, Abuelita,*" said Rodrigo, walking up to my grandmother to give her a hug. The next moment, I heard a crunch.

"Ooh, sorry . . ."

Rodrigo raised his foot and discovered he had just stepped on a chicken head. Without the slightest bit of concern, Rodrigo scraped an eyeball off the bottom of his shoe.

"You look good, Abuelita," Rodrigo said. "Like a teenager."

Abuelita smiled. "Come, get your things and join us inside. I'll introduce you to your cousin."

Rodrigo picked up his bag, scraped a few last remaining bits of chicken brains from his foot, then followed inside. There was only one thing I could say.

"*Sí, Abuelita.*"

chapter dieciocho

Lots of people came for dinner at my grandmother's house that night because in small villages, the first night a relative comes in from El Norte is always a big deal. There were first cousins. There were second cousins. There were third cousins. There were even a few fourth cousins. When you're a Mexican, it seems like everyone is a cousin. We call them *primos*.

Fourteen relatives sat down and began to enjoy the feast. I realized that even though I had been to this *casa* before, I didn't remember that much of it. It had been a long time since I last visited this part of Mexico, and even then it had been for only a few days, back when I was a little girl. Little kids ran around. Old people sipped Dos Equis. I didn't know who was who or what was what. A plate was passed my way.

"*Toma,*" said the man to my left. I paused.

"Go ahead," he continued in Spanish, offering me the plate. "It's Abuelita's famous chicken."

I hesitated, not sure what to do. In the United States, our chicken comes in neatly wrapped packages, not straight out of the backyard, still clucking before some one-tooth warrior with a machete slices off its head. The meal, for me, seemed a little too . . . I don't know, fresh.

"*No, gracias,*" I said. The man paused and gave me a strange look. I think he was some sort of second uncle on my mother's side.

"*Soy vegetariana,*" I said in a low voice. I figured that telling him I was a vegetarian would explain why I didn't want to eat the chicken.

"*¿Una qué?*" the man asked with a puzzled look.

"*Una vegetariana,*" I quietly repeated, not wanting to call attention to myself. For some reason he seemed to have no idea what I was talking about. I guess they didn't have vegetarians in this part of Mexico.

I tried to explain again.

"*Yo soy una . . .*"

"*Pocha,*" a voice rang out from across the table. Everyone laughed at the comment. I looked up. It was *mi prima Maria.*

"*La pocha* feels bad for the chicken," my cousin continued. "Perhaps she thinks we should have set it free so that it could build a new life for itself in El Norte?"

Maria took a bite of a drumstick and continued. "Just wait till she sees the feast we will throw her when she leaves," she added as she chewed her food. "She might need to call immigration."

The table laughed again, this time louder. My cousin Maria was around my age and around my height. I would have said she was pretty, too, if she weren't such a raging bitch.

A *pocha* is what "real" Mexicans who live in Mexico call Mexicans who live in El Norte. They say our Spanish isn't as good, that we act in ways that are not like the old country, and that we're arrogant and conceited because America is our home and we have so much more than they ever will. No, *pocha* is not a curse word, but it's definitely insulting, especially when you are being called it over and over again on your first night in Mexico at a table that is supposed to be filled with *familia*.

"*Aquí, pocha* . . . have some beans. Or maybe American girls don't fart either?"

The table laughed again. Maria was so funny, she should have been a stand-up comedian.

"Well, I can't speak for American girls, but I know American boys do," said Rodrigo, and then he blew out an incredibly loud *BRRRIIPPP!* His fart rumbled like a thunder over a mountain range. For some reason the fact that my brother ripped a big one at the dinner table amused everyone greatly. I looked up and saw smiles all around.

Rodrigo grinned with pride. Ever since we were little, he had always been able to pass gas on demand, like it was some sort of skill to be appreciated or something.

"*Ay, Dios mío*," said the lady seated next to my brother as she waved her hand in front of her nose. "He makes wind like a real Mexican. Almost causes my eyes to water."

Rodrigo smiled then farted again. The table laughed some more. I lowered my eyes and shook my head. I thought this was supposed to be a respectable meal.

Though I'd only been at Abuelita's for a quarter of a day, the urge quickly came over me to leave. It's all I wanted to do. When my cousin Maria called me a *pocha* eight more times at dinner, I wanted to leave. When I took out the gifts I had brought from the United States, and Rodrigo followed me around the room as I handed them out, telling everyone, "These are from me, look what I brought you," even though he hadn't had a dang thing to do with buying or bringing them, I wanted to leave. And when everyone finally went back to their own homes, I wished more than anything that I could do the same. Sometimes Abuelita's house slept fourteen, sometimes it slept two, but for this summer, it looked like there would only be four of us, just me and Abuelita, my cousin Maria, and Rodrigo, the farting wonder boy. It was shaping up to be like some sort of bad reality TV show or something.

"*Me voy,*" said Rodrigo, once the last guest had left.

"*¿A dónde vas?*" I asked, wondering where in the world Rodrigo could be going.

"To meet Carla," he answered.

I wrinkled my forehead. "Who's Carla?" I said.

"You know, from the airplane," Rodrigo answered. "She invited me to a club. I'd invite you, but sorry, no Lame-os." Rodrigo ran his fingers through his greasy hair and, satisfied that he looked good, dashed out the front door.

"*Hasta luego, Abuelita,*" my brother said as he bounced off of the front porch. "*Adios, Maria.*" A moment later, Rodrigo disappeared into the black, desert night as if he had lived here his whole life. How did he even know where to go, I wondered.

I slowly walked onto the front porch, unsure of what to do. Abuelita and my cousin Maria sat in rocking chairs sipping *café* and eating *pan una concha*, a dessert-style bread with sugar on top. Except for all the nature sounds, it was quiet. Now there were just three of us.

"*¿Quieres?*" offered my grandmother. There was an empty chair next to her on the left.

"No," I answered. Unlike some females on this planet, I didn't want to spend the rest of my life on a porch yapping my entire existence away.

"*Pero gracias,*" I added, not wanting to be rude.

"Are you sure, *pocha?*" Maria asked. "It's good."

"No," I said, stepping off the porch. "I'm just going to use *el baño* and then go to bed. Been a long day."

"Suit yourself, *pocha,*" said Maria. I wished she'd stop calling me that.

Abuelita didn't push the point. And she hadn't said a word to Rodrigo either when he left, even though he was dashing off into the middle of the night to do goodness-knows-what with goodness-knows-who. I guess after having had thirteen kids and forty-one grandkids, a person stops micromanaging everyone's behavior. Maybe once upon a time Abuelita had been some sort of wise woman, but tonight all I saw in her was *una vieja*, an old lady who was completely out of touch.

Abuelita reclined in her chair and lit a cigar. Not a cigarette. Not a cigarillo. A cigar. The smell of tobacco filled the air. She blew a smoke ring. I should have figured that she smoked cigars. For all I knew, Abuelita had a penis too. I headed off to the bathroom, thinking more and more about how much I wanted to go home.

"Hey, *pocha*, watch for scorpions," said Maria. "Sometimes they hide under the toilet paper."

I stopped.

"*En serio,*" Maria added. "Out here there's scorpions, and spiders and snakes too."

I looked at Abuelita for a sign to see if *mi prima* was messing around with me or if she was telling the truth. Abuelita rocked back and forth in her chair and blew another smoke ring, not giving me one indication either way if there was reason to be afraid.

"Late at night when I have to go, I usually dig *un poso*," Maria offered.

"A hole?" I said.

"Like a cat. It's safer," she answered. "You could be our *pocha gato.*"

A smile came to Abuelita's face when Maria made

the cat joke. I thought about just holding it in until morning, but there was no way for me not to pee. And usually I got up at least once or twice in the middle of the night too. *Dios mío* what was next, wrestling a rhinoceros when I got my period?

I tippy-toed toward the wooden shed. There was no light once I got inside. I closed the door and sat on the toilet seat in complete dark, terrified that a rattlesnake was going to pop its head up and bite me in the privates. My goal, once I sat down, was to pee fast and leave, but even though I really had to go wee-wee bad, I was too scared to tinkle, so I just sat there on the hard toilet seat with nothing coming out.

I tried to calm down.

Come on, Sonia . . . pee. There could be a hornets' nest.

I gave a good effort but couldn't make anything happen. Then the noises started getting louder. Crickets. Birds. Rustling in the bushes. At any moment I expected there to be a gigantic tarantula headed for my cooch.

A minute later I heard laughter coming from the porch. Obviously, my cousin and grandmother were talking about me. I felt low. In Mexico I was nothing more than a stupid American.

How funny, I thought, because in America I was

nothing more than a stupid Mexican. No matter where I was, I was an outsider.

Finally I tinkled.

After I closed the door to the shed I walked up to the sink by the side of the house, washed my hands, and headed back inside.

"Are you sure you don't want to join us, *pocha*?" asked Maria.

"No," I said.

"You know, around here we have a saying: The porch, it turns everyone into poets," said Abuelita. "Maybe you too are a poet," she added.

"No," I answered. "All I am is tired. Very tired. *Buenas noches*."

I turned to go inside and saw Abuelita staring at me with an intense look on her face. I guess I hadn't noticed before, but my grandmother had deep, penetrating eyes that knew how to stare right into the core of a person. The hazel-colored tint around her pupils almost seemed to glow. After a moment, her look was so intense, I couldn't handle her gaze anymore and broke eye contact. For a second, it felt as if she had just looked into my soul.

Slowly I walked inside.

"*Buenas noches, pocha.*"

"*Buenas noches,*" I said, and closed the door.

chapter diecinueve

Being in the middle of nowhere, I wouldn't have been shocked to have been woken up by a rooster. Or even a chicken. But by an egg?

"*Buenas tardes*," said Abuelita as she stood over me, holding a *huevo*. "Now, let's see what wrong with you."

"Huh? *¿Qué hora es?*" I asked, wanting to know what time it was.

"*Temprano*," she replied, pulling the sheets off of me. "*Muy temprano*."

With one eye open I took a look toward the window. It was still completely dark outside. No duh it was *muy temprano*. The sun wasn't even out yet.

"Come on, get up," she ordered, in Spanish. "No such thing as a lazy Mexican." Abuelita laughed at her joke and pulled me up to a seated position in the bed. When she smiled, the thought crossed my mind that her one remaining tooth looked kind of lonely in her mouth, and I wondered how long it would be before it joined the rest of her other teeth and fell out, too.

"Now, let's find your problem," she said.

"*¿Qué problema?*" I answered, not having any idea what she was talking about. "There's nothing wrong with me. Please, Abuelita, one more hour of sleep."

"*Soy una curandera,*" she explained as she began to do all sorts of weird motions over my head with the egg. "Let's see if I can fix you."

I had heard about this superstitious witch doctor stuff before, but I'd never actually seen it in real life. Something about how *curanderas* could move an egg over your body and then crack it in a glass to identify your sickness. Supposedly, if the egg yolk settled at the bottom of the glass, everything was fine. If the egg floated, the *curandera* would know how to read the yolk, see what signs were present, and then take steps to choose what herbs would best cure the problem. If you ask me, it was just a bunch of mumbo jumbo. Give me a doctor with a stethoscope and some X-ray machines any day of the week.

"*Por favor, Abuelita . . .*" I pleaded. But even though Abuelita wasn't a physically big woman, she was the type of old lady that not even a 350-pound truck driver could say no to, and she continued waving an egg over my head, my ears, and my arms in some kind of prayerlike fashion. The egg didn't seem very holy to me—it was just a regular old egg—but Abuelita was very, very serious about the whole process. I decided to just let her do her thing. The quicker she finished, the quicker I could go back to bed.

Abuelita took her time. She waved the egg. She listened to the egg. She talked to the egg. And for some reason, this kooky old woman thought that the egg was going to talk back. As she went on and on, I hoped the egg, if it was going to say anything, would mention that I needed more sleep. This was getting ridiculous.

Abuelita moved the egg across my throat, over my heart, then paused. I looked down. The egg was trembling. She watched as the egg shook, almost as if something were happening on the inside of the shell. Abuelita raised her eyes to look at me.

Was something wrong?

She didn't speak. Instead she looked back at the egg and paid careful attention to its every tremble. Slowly she began to move the egg over my stomach.

Then it exploded!

Egg yolk splattered on my chest, sprayed across my thighs, and landed in my hair. Goopy, yellow egg yolk even dripped from my chin. Gross!

"Abuelita," I said, "why'd you squeeze it?" I was sitting in such a big mess I didn't even know where to begin to start cleaning myself up.

"I did not squeeze it," she replied.

"Ugh . . . Look at this."

"But I have located your problem."

"What problem?" I said. "*Yo no tengo un problema* other than there is egg all over me."

"*Mija,*" said Abuelita. She reached out and softly touched my arm. "*Es serio.*"

I raised my eyes. *Serious?*

"You hold something inside. Deep inside. But it grows."

Abuelita paused. For the first time, she didn't seem four hundred years old anymore.

"And soon, if you do not deal with it, it will . . ." Her voice trailed off and she didn't finish the sentence.

"It will what?" I asked.

She took a moment before answering, then looked at me with eyes that seemed to glow.

"It will, like the egg, explode."

Abuelita bowed her head, rose from my bed, and

left. She didn't offer any advice. She didn't offer any herbs. She didn't offer an ear to speak to or a shoulder to cry on. All she did was offer the facts and leave.

I sat alone in wet, yolky egg drippings, wondering what she was talking about. Suddenly an idea came to me. I bit my lower lip and paused.

"No," I said to myself, pushing the idea out of my brain. "Can't be."

A moment later I climbed out of bed, stripped off my clothes, and went to clean myself up.

Good thing I didn't believe in all that mumbo jumbo egg stuff, I thought to myself. I stopped and caught a glance of myself in the mirror.

Whoa, I looked horrible. Really horrible.

"Yeah, good thing," I told myself a second time.

After washing up, I went to the kitchen where Maria was preparing some food while Abuelita added a small log to the fire roaring underneath an old-fashioned, wood-burning stove. The two of them moved quietly yet purposefully. There was no conversation. I helped myself to a banana.

Maria hurriedly finished her task, scooped up her things, and headed for the door.

"*Me voy,*" she said. "I'll be back after lunch."

"*Llévate a Sonia,*" Abuelita said, not looking up.

Maria paused, obviously not happy about what she'd just been told. It was clear she didn't want to take me with her. Heck, I didn't want to go anywhere anyway, especially with her. However, Maria knew better than to talk back to her grandmother. If Abuelita said to take me, she would be taking me.

Maria turned and scowled. "Come, *pocha*. And grab those," she said, nodding to a pile of clothes on the floor.

"What?" I asked. "Where? Can I at least shower first?"

"Shower?" she said. "Don't worry, we'll shower. But *apúrate*; Abuelita smells the rain."

I looked at Abuelita to see if I really had to go, but she didn't look up from under the stove.

"*Ahorita*, *pocha*, didn't you hear me? Abuelita smells the rain." And with that, Maria zipped out of the room, carrying a bag of food and a pile of clothes. I eyed the pile she had ordered me to take. Mine was much bigger than hers.

Figures, I thought.

"I'll meet you outside," she said. She left the kitchen and disappeared.

I paused and looked again to Abuelita for an explanation, but my grandmother still didn't lift her head from under the stove. It seemed that she was intent on building the perfect fire. I stood there like an idiot for ten seconds, not knowing what to do. Finally I grabbed the pile of clothes Maria had pointed to and went to meet my cousin out front.

Great, my new best friend and I were off to do the laundry. No breakfast. No coffee. No shower. Cinderella was back, south-of-the-border style.

Maria exited the house, and suddenly I discovered I was wrong. It was not going to be just me and my new best friend on this little journey. It was going to be me and my new best friend and her ten-month-old baby daughter, Isabella.

Maria was a mother?

Goodness, my cousin couldn't have been more than seventeen. The only thing I could think of was that the baby had been asleep last night in the other room when everyone was over for dinner. But sleeping through all that noise?

Maria tossed her daughter into an old-fashioned pouch, slung it over her back, and grabbed the pile of laundry. With the baby, the food, two bottles of water strapped around her neck, and her own pile of laundry under her arm, the amount Maria was carrying had suddenly grown to twice the size of my stuff. She didn't complain, though. Or ask me to share more of the load. I would have at least carried a water bottle, but she didn't say a word. Obviously, Maria was the hardheaded type.

We began walking.

The morning sun rose over the mountains. Fresh, frosty breath blew from my mouth. Dew dripped off the grass. I guess it would have been a beautiful scene if I wasn't being forced to experience it with a person who hated my guts. We moved along in total silence, the baby as quiet as a plastic doll the whole way.

As we hiked farther and farther along, I became more convinced that this whole "wisdom of the elders" thing was completely overrated. I mean, first Abuelita breaks an egg on me at four o'clock in the morning, then she scares me into thinking that I have some sort of "deep" problem, and now I'm walking to a river to hurry up and do laundry before the rain comes, which, by the way, she had smelled.

I looked up. There wasn't a cloud in the sky.

Didn't Abuelita know that times had changed and the world now was a place filled with the Internet, text messaging, and downloading music? Walking to rivers to do laundry was something that people had done a thousand years ago. Hadn't anyone down here ever heard of Maytag?

It was a really long walk to where we were going, and as we moved along without conversation, I realized more and more how much I hated the mentality of the people down here. Sure, to my cousin I was a *pocha*, nothing more than an arrogant, stuck-up American, but to me, Maria was a small-town, oppressed little village girl. I mean, she already had a baby (with no father around, of course), and in my eyes—my *pocha* eyes—Maria was yet another victim of Mexican poverty and oppression. No education. No money. No hope for any kind of good job. No nothing.

As Isabella bounced in her pouch on her mother's back, I wondered if Maria had gotten knocked up during a one-night stand, or whether she'd had a short relationship with a *novio* that ended with her getting pregnant and the father bailing, like so many guys do, not wanting to take responsibility for a child that was half his.

Maybe he was one of those wolves who was about twenty-five years old and had told Maria that he was really sixteen and he'd love her forever just so he could pluck her cherry like the wolf-boys do back in America. As we continued along, I thought about how *mi prima* might as well be living in the eleventh century. I mean, jeez, she'd probably never even been on the Internet before.

Isabella sure was quiet, though. She hardly made a

peep. The baby just bounced along on her mommy's back as if she didn't have a care in the world. After a few more minutes of my cousin not talking to me, I decided to hang back and take a closer look at her daughter.

Isabella looked up, and her beauty caught me off guard. Wow, was she cute. Of course, most babies are cute, but this baby was really cute, like with big, brown eyes and a perfect nose and thin, pretty lips. I smiled. Isabella smiled back. Her smile made my smile grow even bigger.

Yep, I thought. Though I would never tell it to *mi prima*, this baby was gorgeous. I made a funny face, and the baby giggled. What a great laugh, I thought.

"Hi there, cutie-pie," I said to Isabella as we cruised along. "Hello there, gorgeous." I spoke in English because I had heard that it was good to expose babies to as many languages as possible, because their brains are like sponges and languages will soak in. Some English would be good for her, I thought.

"Are you a happy baby?" I asked. *"Goo-goo-ga-ga?"* Isabella turned her head and stared off at the passing trees. "Hey, Isabella," I said, trying to grab her attention. "Isabella, look, over here," I said. "Look."

She didn't look.

"Isabella . . . over here." I switched to Spanish to see if that would work. *"Hola, bebe . . . mira aquí . . . Isabella . . ."*

She still didn't look. I guess she didn't know her name yet.

"No use talking to her, *pocha*."

No use? That's kind of harsh, I thought. I mean, just because Maria didn't like me didn't mean that I couldn't talk to her baby, did it? After all, wasn't I like some sort of aunt or something?

"Yap all you want," Maria continued. "She'll never hear you."

How rude, I thought. It was obvious that Maria was the type of mom who—

"She's deaf," Maria added, interrupting my train of thought.

I paused. "Deaf?" I said.

"Yeah, you know, deaf. She can't hear. You've heard of it, haven't you?" Maria said in a snippy tone of voice.

I stared at Isabella as she bounced happily along.

"Like I said, talk all you want, but she's never going to hear."

Maria made a left and followed the trail as it moved downhill. I followed, but the silence between us became thicker. A thousand thoughts raced through my mind, all of them sad.

Deaf? How horrible, I thought. Probably didn't get immunized. Children not having proper immunization was still a big issue with people who lived in poverty, and everyone knew that serious problems could develop when kids didn't get their shots.

As we marched along, the anger inside of me started to grow. They should require people to have a license to have a kid, or something, I thought. I mean, some folks are just not fit.

We finally arrived at the river, and before I knew it, I was washing clothing on rocks like they had done back in the Stone Age. Maria stood next to me, knee-deep in water as we both dunked and slapped clothes against big stones, scrubbing the dirt out of the cotton fabrics with small bars of soap. Maria made a few hand signs at Isabella as she sat on a blanket in the shade, playing with a cup and spoon. Isabella was the most content baby I'd ever seen. Happy. Fun-loving. Quiet. Then again, she was still too young to know how hard she would have it later on in life. A deaf, poor, fatherless Mexican girl living in a home with no money . . . Come on, how many more strikes could a person have against them?

Enjoy it while you can, baby, I thought as I

watched Isabella bang things together. Enjoy it while you can.

After about forty-five minutes of scrubbing in *silencio*, Maria finished with her pile and looked to inspect the clothes and bedding I was washing. I think she expected to find a half-assed job, but I never do anything half-assed, especially when it comes to cleaning, and I was sure that the things I had scrubbed were spick-and-span. She checked out my clothes with a close, scrutinizing eye, then turned away without saying a word. A moment later, she stripped off her shirt and bra and dunked her tits in the water.

It caught me totally by surprise.

Maria's breasts were full and perfectly shaped. She had dark round nipples and a firm lean stomach. I couldn't help but stare, her body was so beautiful. A moment after that, she grabbed a bottle of shampoo, stripped down to her thong, and began bathing herself, top to bottom, then up, over, and under. When she was finished washing her hair, she took off her underwear, washed them and the rest of the clothes she had been wearing, then walked naked to the shore, where she spread everything out to dry and sat down on the blanket.

A moment later she scooped up Isabella and began to breast-feed. Isabella rolled her head, opened her mouth, and began happily sucking on Mommy's booby. It was time for lunch.

Maria cradled her daughter and relaxed, enjoying the soft wind against her uncovered body. She looked like some kind of Latina goddess.

I finished up washing the last of my clothes. Suddenly I heard a splash in the river next to me. It was a bottle of shampoo.

"Bathe, *pocha* . . . then we'll eat."

I hesitated. I had never bathed in a river before. What if someone came along?

I looked around. A lot of things could be said about where we were, but heavily populated was not one of them. We hadn't seen another person all morning.

Maria stared at me. I was sure it was a test to see if I thought I was too good to bathe in a river. Her, she'd probably bathed this way for years. Me, I'd always had a tub and a bath mat and a door to close.

Maybe I was a *pocha*?

I stripped off my top. Screw her, I thought. Even if I was a *pocha*, I wasn't going to admit it.

I got naked, dunked my tits, and took my first river bath. It was awkward, but I did my best to pretend it was no big deal. Maria occasionally looked over to check my progress, and I acted as if I had been bathing this way my whole life. At one point I even whistled like I was on a relaxing vacation.

Just another day for me, I pretended. *River baths and before-dawn egg therapy. Yep, scrub-a-dub-dub . . . just another regular old day for me.*

Finally I finished and climbed to the shore. Maybe I had bathed in the river, but sitting nude on a blanket while eating lunch next to my naked cousin was way too ancient Maya for me. Surprisingly, Maria reached into her bag and tossed me a shirt and pair of pants. The top was thin and white, the pants tan and light-weight. It was typical of what most people in this part of the country wear on a warm day. I guess Maria had thought ahead to bring a dry outfit for me.

I looked at the clothing.

"Gracias," I said.

She didn't answer. Instead she took Isabella off her breast, burped her, and then reached into a basket and laid out tortillas, roasted peppers, cheese, beans, and fruits.

"Eat," she said, taking a bite of an apple. "Time to eat."

I reached for a pepper. It was delicious, the best pepper I'd ever had. The flavor lit up my mouth as if I were eating a piece of sunshine.

On the one hand I kind of wanted to talk to *mi*

prima, but on the other hand I didn't. I wasn't sure what I had done to make Maria so angry and rude to me. Really, I was just being who I just naturally was.

Then I realized, so was she. I took a small bite of an orange. We ate in silence, both of us hardheaded and stubborn, like mules refusing to speak to one another. Finally, when the food was done and our meal was finished, we packed our things and returned to *la casa de Abuelita*.

Minutes after we walked onto the front porch, I heard a crash of thunder. Then the rain began.

chapter veinte

We put the laundry on a clothesline underneath the back porch to dry to avoid the rain. Then Isabella took a nap. So did Maria. *Siestas* in Mexico are still a tradition, and considering how early I had gotten up, I thought it seemed like a good idea for me to take a nap too.

Only thing was, I couldn't sleep.

I lay in bed tossing and turning, with wild, scary thoughts running through my brain. My mind was like a hyped-up monkey leaping from branch to branch. Deaf babies, ignorant village girls, crazy grandmothers, stupid eggs, and people at home I didn't want to think about kept popping into my mind. I got out of bed, needing something to distract me.

Unfortunately, there was no TV, no computer, no

anything in this house. Just a couple of books. How in the world did these people function, I thought. I walked out to the front porch, sat down in one of the rocking chairs, and stared out at the mountains.

Bo-ring.

I went back inside.

Where is Abuelita? I thought. Aw, with her, who knew? Maybe she had walked to the moon for some cheese.

I went to the kitchen but wasn't really hungry, so I went back outside. A person was approaching the property. Good, I thought. Some company. Then I realized I must be getting desperate. Was I really excited to see Rodrigo?

"Where've you been?" I asked when he stepped onto the porch, wet from the rain.

"You mean, 'Who've I been in?'" he replied with a smirk. "I love Mexico. The bitches down here think I'm a rock star."

A rock star? Dios mío.

It turns out that Rodrigo had gone down to a local bar to meet the stewardess and watch the Mexican national *fútbol* team play El Salvador. Mexico and El Salvador were fierce rivals, and the game had gone into double overtime. Rodrigo had drunk until he could hardly see, sung the Mexican national anthem with forty or fifty new friends, had his drinks paid for all night by people he had never met, and then, after Mexico won on a header goal off a corner kick in the 107th minute, my brother was taken home by some fake blonde—nope, not the stewardess—whose name he didn't even know.

"She banged my brains out, fed me breakfast, then banged me again," he said with a smile.

"This is more than I want to know," I told him.

"Then she made me leave before her husband got home. He works the night shift at some factory."

"You slept with a married woman?"

"And there were at least six other females I could have hooked up with last night," he said. "Did I mention how much I love this country?"

I stared at him in disbelief.

"What?" he asked.

"You're a pig," I said.

Rodrigo snorted, not caring one bit what I thought. "Any more of that cake around?"

"You better watch it, Rigo" I told him. "*Hombres* find out you are messing with their wives, they get crazy down here."

"Bah," he said. "Time for *siesta*. Gotta rest up for tonight." He stretched his arms and yawned.

"Hey, you wanna come? You know, see the

town?" he asked. "Oh wait, I forgot. No Lame-os."

Rodrigo chuckled, walked to his room, and flopped onto his bed without even taking off his wet T-shirt.

"Wake me when there's food," he said. A few minutes later he was snoring.

For the next five days, Rodrigo followed the same pattern, and with any luck—at least in his mind—he was going to spend his entire summer this way: drinking, sleeping with local girls, and watching *fútbol* at the bar. Abuelita's house was the perfect training ground for him to turn into the man of his dreams: a jobless, brown-skinned, *puta*-chasing boozer.

As for me, I was quickly being turned into a typical, young Mexican girl. Every morning I was up bright and early for chores: dishes, dusting, sweeping, and cleaning. Keeping a neat house was very important to Abuelita, and since I was spending the summer, I had to do my fair share of the work in the a.m. hours. I guess it was okay to expect me to help, even though Rodrigo didn't have to do a damn thing. The whole boy/girl unfair culture thing was total BS, but I didn't say a word. At least the chores gave me something to do. Other than that, Mexico was incredibly boring. My afternoons were totally free.

Maria, on the other hand, was always in motion, morning, noon, and night. Isabella might have napped the first day I was in town, but after that, she was all squiggles and squirms and motoring around to explore the universe without hardly any napping at all. And Isabella not napping meant that Maria practically never had a chance to sit down. Diapers, washing spit-up, changing clothes, monitoring Isabella while she tried to put everything she touched into her mouth. Watching Maria made me realize just how much hard work it was having a child, especially with no help. Once, as the baby played with an old deck of cards, I saw Maria fall asleep while leaning against a wall. I really thought *mi prima* was going to fall over and bonk her head, but she caught herself before she fell. Every day she looked more and more exhausted.

Maria caught me witnessing this side of her and I could tell she felt embarrassed. *Mi prima* was turning into an old maid right before my eyes.

I finally stopped even trying to lay my head down for afternoon naps because incredibly unsettling thoughts about all the things wrong in the world would race through my mind, and they bothered me way too much to sleep. One afternoon, looking for something to do, anything to distract me, I walked over to the bookshelf. Much to my surprise, I got lucky and found something of interest: a big thick wedding album.

I have always been a sucker for weddings, so I put the album under my arm and went to look at it on the front porch. It'd be cool to see my grandfather, I thought. And Abuelita as a young girl. I bet she had teeth back then. I opened the first page to see what Abuelita had looked like before her 250th birthday.

Page one shocked me. I'd expected to find a young bride with a handsome groom standing at the altar of an old church. And that's what I did find. Except Abuelita wasn't the bride.

Maria was.

I turned the page. The groom was very handsome. As I flipped through more of the wedding album, I saw people dressed in nice clothing, smiling and obviously having a wonderful time. Mexican weddings were always incredible *fiestas*, but Maria's wedding looked like something out of a fairy tale. There was food and flowers and cake and relatives and dancing and music and a whole lot of love oozing off of the page. It was clear that this event had been a magnificent occasion. They were a gorgeous couple, too, Maria and her groom, like a match made in heaven.

But if Maria was married, I thought, where was . . .

"Es bonita, sí?" said a voice, interrupting my train of thought.

I looked up. *"Sí, verdaderamente,"* I said, it was

pretty. "But, Abuelita, if Maria is married, where is her husband?"

I paused then answered my own question. *"¿El Norte?"*

Abuelita didn't answer right away. Instead, she sat down in the rocking chair next to me.

"Sí y no," she answered. *"Sí y no."*

"No comprendo," I replied. What did she mean, 'yes and no'?

Abuelita then proceeded to tell me Maria's story.

Maria's husband, the groom in the pictures, was named Juan Carlos. His plan had been to become a civil engineer. Though he had graduated high school and was offered a special scholarship to go to college in America, Juan Carlos had chosen to enroll at the prestigious Universidad Nacional Autónoma de México in Mexico City.

"If all our best leave," he had said, "who will be left to stay?"

Juan Carlos loved Mexico. And he was very proud of his country. Sure, there were things wrong with it, but there were things wrong with every country, he'd said. He had no desire to go north.

Especially because he was madly in love.

From the moment he'd met Maria, Juan Carlos had known she was the one and only true love of his life. His parents, however, disliked the idea of their marriage very much.

"There are plenty of fish in the sea," they'd told him. "You have the chance to become something. Something great. Love can wait."

It was true that Juan Carlos could have had his choice of many, many girls. He was handsome, at the top of his class, and quite clearly he had a bright future. His parents couldn't understand why he wanted to marry a *pobrecita* like Maria when he so easily could have spent his life with the daughter of someone wealthy and important.

Abuelita reached across the table and poured herself a glass of tea.

"*¿Quieres?*" she asked.

The drink looked good.

"*Sí,*" I replied. Abuelita poured me a glass of tea, and I reclined in the rocking chair.

Hey, I thought, this is kinda comfortable. I rocked back and forth a few times and sipped the tea, which had been sweetened with some sort of flower—hibiscus, maybe. It tasted nice.

"*Gracias,*" I replied.

"*De nada,*" my grandmother answered. A moment later she continued her story.

Juan Carlos, she explained, didn't care about

status. Or his family's wishes. Or their high hopes for him as their only child. All he cared about was the beautiful little village girl who had stolen his heart. They were married one and a half years after they'd met.

Abuelita told me that it wasn't Maria his parents didn't like; it was her family tree they didn't approve of. They even said that the only reason Maria's parents liked Juan Carlos so much was because he would one day become their meal ticket.

"You mean, his parents told Maria's parents that they were gold diggers?" I asked.

"*Sí*, the day after the wedding," replied Abuelita. "And Maria's father, my son, is a very proud man. So proud that he soon left for El Norte to make a better life for his remaining kids and wife. After Juan Carlos's parents accused him of being money hungry, he felt he had no choice."

Too much pride, I thought.

"Yes, too much pride," said Abuelita, as if she had read my mind. She looked at me with wise, glowing eyes. A moment later, after another sip of tea, she continued.

"Juan Carlos told his parents that if he had to choose between his new family and his old, his new family would win every time, and he vowed not to speak to them until they apologized to Maria and her parents.

"Did they?" I asked.

"Of course not. Soon Isabella was born. Then the baby got sick."

"Was she immunized?" I asked.

Abuelita stared at me long and hard. "We may be poor, but stupid we are not."

I lowered my eyes and felt bad. It was a *pocha* question.

What the baby needed, Abuelita explained, was medicine. Expensive medicine. The sickness went beyond anything that Abuelita as a *curandera* could heal and Juan Carlos refused to ask his parents for even a peso. Finally, with the baby growing more and more ill, Juan Carlos did the only thing he could—he headed for the border to make some quick money in *Los Estados Unidos*. In Mexico, Juan Carlos could make about two dollars a day for his labor, but in America he could make over fifteen dollars—and that was just for one hour. Plus, Juan Carlos spoke English and had a very good head on his shoulders. With a little luck, he could be in and out of El Norte in two weeks, with five hundred dollars in his pocket—more than enough to buy his daughter what she needed. It was a sum that would have taken him months to earn in Mexico.

"And months his baby did not have," said Abuelita. It was an easy decision. Juan Carlos kissed his wife and baby good-bye. "After that," she said, "well, only rumors are known."

Abuelita stopped. It was the end of her story. She took another sip of her tea, rocked in her chair, and looked out on the hills.

I waited.

"The rain will not be back for a while," she said thoughtfully.

"What rumors, Abuelita?" I demanded. "What is it they think happened to Maria's husband?"

Slowly she turned.

"Something not good," she answered. "Something not good."

Supposedly, a fight with the *policía* had ensued in the desert. Juan Carlos had refused to hire *coyotes* for his journey because he was a single man in good physical shape who only needed to carry a small pack on his back. Wasting precious money on hiring illegal guides to escort him across the border made little sense to him.

But *coyotes* do more than just act as guides. They also prearrange for the *policía* to be bribed, and when the *federales* caught Juan Carlos on the Mexican side of the border about to sneak across into El Norte, they demanded a bribery payment. They weren't enforcing any laws, they were simply trying to fill their own corrupt pockets.

"And Juan Carlos refused to pay?" I asked.

"Of course," she answered.

Years ago, Abuelita explained, the *policía* might have let a single man like Juan Carlos through without too much of a problem, but with the recent crackdowns from America, bribing the *policía* had become much more necessary.

The *policía* knew that if they let one person get through without paying, soon two would get through. Then three. And before anyone realized it, one hundred would be getting through without paying, and the *policía* had families to feed.

"And tequila habits too," Abuelita added.

Supposedly, Juan Carlos had argued with the *policía* about "exploiting their own" and about how Mexico needed to rise up above the corruption so that it could move forward as a nation and change for the better. Juan Carlos was a smart, proud man who gave a very noble speech, it was said.

Five weeks later his body was found in a dry river gulch by the Arizona border. Isabella survived the illness but ended up going deaf. The parents of Juan Carlos said they wanted nothing to do with the bastard child and blamed Maria for their son's death. Maria, of course, refuses to take Isabella to El Norte to be reunited with her own parents, because Juan Carlos would have wanted her to stay in Mexico and raise her daughter here, in a way that would one day make society proud.

Abuelita paused. It seemed that even the wind had stopped blowing.

"All he wanted was to make some money for his sick baby and then return home. Now," she said, "he's just another dead *vato*, another brown-skin who died in the desert with a story no one will ever hear."

I felt a lump in my throat.

"And Maria and her baby," Abuelita said, "for now they live with me."

chapter veintiuno

The next afternoon was warm, with scattered clouds.

"I could watch her," I said.

Maria didn't turn around.

"Serious," I offered. "I'd like to. Maybe you could, you know . . . *tomar una siesta.*"

Maria was folding a pile of baby clothes that Isabella had just playfully unfolded. For the first time, I saw a look in my cousin's eye that made her seem, I don't know . . . vulnerable.

Isabella covered her face with a pair of tiny pants and played peekaboo with me. When I grinned, she smiled.

"Really, I want to," I said as I crossed the room and scooped up the baby without asking permission. "Your daughter, she's smart and so beautiful."

Isabella reached out, grabbed my earring, and

started to play with the hoop. "And it certainly doesn't seem like either of us want to nap right now anyway."

Like her baby, Maria had big brown eyes. They became wet with tears, though I could see my cousin was doing her best to stop them from falling. I picked up a pack of counting cards Isabella seemed to greatly enjoy.

"We can study math or something," I said, trying to sound cheery.

Maria didn't move.

"Go, Maria," I said. "It's okay. Go."

"You been talking to Abuelita?" she asked.

I paused, not exactly sure of what to say.

"You're a good mother, *prima*," I said, then paused. "And truthfully, I don't know where you find the strength. This little *nena* has many needs." I looked at the baby, then raised my eyes to my cousin. "But so do you."

Maria looked me in the eyes as if she were searching for permission to accept my help.

"You're stronger than I am, *prima*." I said. "But even the strong sometimes need help from those who they think are weak."

I shifted the baby in my arms. "Do you want to spend a bit of time with Tía Sonia?" I asked. "That's right," I said in a baby voice, *"soy Tía Sonia."*

Isabella's face shined with a big, wide smile. Tears began to fall from Maria's eyes.

"I am not so strong, *pocha*," Maria said. "I still cry every night." She put down the clothes she had been folding, turned, and headed for the door.

"Every fucking night," she said in English.

The door closed behind her.

Later, I found Maria napping on the couch. She hadn't said yes, she hadn't said no, but somehow I had unofficially become Tiá Siesta, the aunt who would take over watching the baby while *mi prima* rested in the middle of warm, breezy, lazy Mexican afternoons.

It quickly became the favorite part of my day.

"Do you mind watching her for a little more?" Maria asked one afternoon as I sat on the floor making the baby laugh with a sock I was using as a puppet. "I want to bathe."

"Sure," I answered. "I could even walk down to the river with you, if you want."

"The river?" Maria replied. "Who bathes down there?"

I paused.

"I do it up here in the shower shed, don't you?"

"You mean . . ."

A smile crossed Maria's face. "Welcome to Mexico . . . *pocha*."

I hesitated, then smiled back. For the first time, Maria and I shared a laugh.

"Did you like the way I tried to dry myself like some sort of mermaid?" Maria asked. "Can I tell you how bad my *tetas* got sunburned that afternoon?"

I giggled.

"Hey, I'm going into town later," she said. "You wanna come? I need to get some things for the baby and check my e-mail."

"Uh, yeah, sure," I answered. "Sounds good."

It turned out that one of Juan Carlos's old friends came by every Tuesday and Friday to take Maria and the baby into town to do errands. I thought that was nice. And though he drove a pickup truck, he didn't make me sit in the back listening to a psycho pooch lick its balls either. That was even nicer.

"*Hasta luego,*" the boy said with a wide smile once we arrived in town.

"Bye, *gracias*," I replied with a friendly wave.

"See you in two hours, Ignacio," Maria said as she closed the door. He drove away. "You see that?" she asked.

"See what?" I said.

"Ignacio," she answered. "He likes you. Probably

wants to do the in-and-out with you before you go back to El Norte."

"Stop," I said.

"Why? You have a *novio*?" asked Maria.

I reached over and brushed a bit of hair out of Isabella's eyes, avoiding the question.

"You do, don't you?" said Maria. "I can tell. What's he like?"

"I don't," I said.

"Liar," she answered. "I can tell, your heart flutters for someone."

"There's no one," I said.

"Sure thing, *pocha*. Sure thing."

We walked into an air-conditioned Internet café and sat at a table. I ordered an orange juice and fed Isabella a banana while Maria checked her e-mail and sent out a few messages. Our table was by a window at the front of the café. It was my first real view of town.

The first thing I noticed was that traffic lanes didn't seem to mean anything. People drove anywhere there were no cars, that was the only rule. If there was no one to the left, they went left. If no one was on the right, they drove right. If there was no one on the sidewalk, they drove on the sidewalk.

These drivers are crazy, I thought. Then I looked to the left.

"Hey, what's that big line across the street for?" I asked.

Maria looked over. There must have been at least 150 women standing against a wall, waiting to enter a store.

"It's Friday, payday," Maria explained. "Today's the day the *vatos* in the United States send their money home."

I stared at the ladies waiting their turn for wire transfers to arrive from the U.S.

"Are there always so many?" I asked.

"No," Maria answered. "Tomorrow, on Saturday, there will be more."

More, I thought. *Mi prima* didn't even look up from the computer screen.

When Maria finished, we exited the café and walked past the long line of women. I stared at them. Tall, short, fat, skinny, they all looked different, yet they all looked the same, as though poverty had created the same kind of wrinkles for each one of them. All that lettuce picking in the States, all those dishes being washed, all those lawns being mowed, and all those gardens being tended to . . . so this is where the men sent their wages, to the women down here, the women who, without American dollars, would not survive.

"Hey, look . . ." Maria suddenly said.

Maria turned Isabella so that she could see a group of barefoot children across the street. They were flying kites. Actually, they weren't kites like American kites; they were pieces of string wrapped around june bugs that danced in the sky at the end of small strands of rope.

A giant smile came to Isabella's face. She stared at the barefoot boys with wide, amazed eyes. I looked on in wonder, too. I had never seen such a thing. The june bugs fluttered and flittered in a way that made them almost hypnotic to watch, and the boys seemed to greatly love what they were doing.

Watching the boys play with their bugs made me think about my brothers back home. The kids here may not have had money, but they made due with what they had without complaining. My brothers at home were always sitting around the house, playing violent video games and whining about how they needed more of this or more of that while they drank soda pop and ate chips. I couldn't even remember the last time my brothers played outside without a Game Boy in their hands. The boys here didn't even have shoes.

Suddenly I realized, if only a few small things had happened differently, those would be my brothers out there flying june bug kites. And that might be me standing in line waiting for U.S. dollars to be sent home from El Norte.

Wow, I thought, what would my life have been like if my parents had not jumped the border? I couldn't even imagine.

"Hey, *pocha . . . pocha*, you ready? We still have a few errands to run."

"*Sí,*" I said, waking from my daze. I looked back at the boys with the june bug kites and the women with wrinkled faces waiting in a line that seemed to stretch on forever.

"Yes," I said. "I'm ready. Let's go."

chapter veintidós

Maria and I became inseparable. We cooked, we cleaned, we walked in the hills, and we laughed about things like doing the in-and-out with Ignacio and about how we needed to feed Rodrigo some butt glue so he would stop farting all the time. And as crazy as it sounds, sitting on the porch became enjoyable for me. Very enjoyable. I had grown to love rocking chairs.

"Hey, Abuelita, how come you had so many children?" Maria asked one night after dinner as we rocked and relaxed in the soft, warm breeze.

"What else is there to do here?" Abuelita answered. "*Nada*, so we make woop-woop to pass the time."

My grandmother smiled with a grin that showed her one tooth. Maria and I couldn't help but laugh.

"What was he like?" Maria asked.

"Your grandfather? Oh, he was good in bed. Had very strong legs so he could pump a long time."

"No, Abuelita, as a person," Maria responded, shaking her head. "As a person, you dirty old bird, what was he like? I never met him."

"Oh, as a person. Honorable," my grandmother replied. "Very honorable. Never told a lie. *Nunca*. He passed quietly in his sleep. It was a good death."

"Do you miss him?" I asked.

Abuelita looked off into the distance and paused. Slowly she took a puff off her cigar.

"He used to smoke these," she said. "And when he passed, we had so many in the drawer, I . . . well, the smoke rings, I guess they are my little way of remembering."

She blew another puff.

"Each one is a valentine."

It was quiet for a moment. Rain began to fall.

"I'll be with him again, though," she added. "People think death divides, but it reunites, too."

Abuelita turned to Maria. I didn't notice that she had started crying.

"Don't worry, *mija*, you'll be with your love again as well," Abuelita said to my cousin. "One day, when your work down here is done, you'll be reunited with your Juan Carlos. You must not lose faith. Some things in this world, they have been written."

The tears fell from Maria's eyes without her even bothering to wipe them. For the next few minutes the sound of raindrops plopping on the roof filled the night air. My heart grew heavy.

"The sky sobs," I said.

"¿*Qué?*" asked Maria.

"The sky cries. And the hills are filled with stories, and the clouds, when they hear the sad tales, they cry too." I looked out at the mountains. "But it's a beautiful sadness," I said. "A beautiful sadness."

A tear began to form in my heart for all the *mujeres de México*. I had never realized how much loneliness there was in the hearts of my people, especially the women. Or how much strength there was to go on, in spite of everything they faced. Maria looked at Abuelita and smiled.

"What?" I said.

"The porch," my cousin answered. "Like Abuelita says, eventually it turns everyone into a poet."

A small grin came to my face, and each of us took a sip of hot tea. It was the prettiest rainfall I had ever seen, and I never wanted it to stop.

Over the next few weeks I learned about the history of *mi familia*, I discovered the magic of the countryside, and I saw firsthand the kindness, courage, and intelligence of my people in a way I had never known. Eight weeks passed as if it were one, and before I realized, it was time to return home.

"But please, no feast, Abuelita," I said.

"Why not?" Maria asked. "*Pocha* still scared of chickens?"

"No," I said with a grin. "I just want a quiet night. A night with"—I paused—"*mi familia.*"

I looked at Isabella as she put a toy bunny rabbit in her mouth. She must have sensed me watching her because suddenly, she looked up and smiled.

"Just *familia*," I repeated.

A last quiet night with Abuelita, Maria, and Isabella would be enough for me. Besides, Rodrigo wouldn't care. He'd spent so much time getting drunk in town, I was sure his final evening would most certainly be at the local bar.

"Okay," Abuelita agreed. "We'll make tamales."

Tamales? A grin came to my face.

"What, you don't like tamales, *pocha*? What are you, a *gabacha*?"

"No," I answered with a laugh. "Tamales sound great."

Each ingredient started from scratch. Each tortilla was rolled by hand, each filling was accompanied by a story, each spice was inserted with either a laugh or a cry or a piece of timeless wisdom. By the time we were done preparing the food, every tamale had been filled to the tippy-top with love, and it turned out to be the most delicious meal I had ever eaten. When we were done, the only thing I wanted was to hold baby Isabella in my arms. I wanted to hold her in my arms forever.

Though you are usually not supposed to wake a sleeping baby, Maria allowed me to take Isabella from her bed and rock her gently in my arms as a final night's treat. I started singing her a song, a lullaby in English.

"I know she can't hear me," I said to Maria in the middle of my song. "But also, I know she can. Does that make sense?"

"It makes perfect sense," Abuelita answered as she lit a cigar. "Perfect sense."

Isabella fell back asleep in my arms as if she were my own.

"You sad, *pocha*?" asked Maria a few minutes later.

I looked up with wet eyes. "I don't want to go."

"Don't be stupid, yes you do."

"But I could stay," I replied. "I mean, I could help you and the baby and . . ."

"You must go!" she snapped. "You must go and

seize the opportunity." My cousin stared at me with fierceness. "It is not an option, you must go."

Maria came over and took the baby from my arms. Her message was clear: I must leave to make something good of myself for all those who can't.

I turned to Abuelita. She rocked back and forth and took a puff off of her cigar. Of course, she didn't say a word.

After a tense moment I stood, walked over to Maria, and gave her a hug. We may have started the summer as cousins who didn't know each other, but we were ending it as more than just *primas*. . . . We were *hermanas*, sisters.

I squeezed her more tightly than I had ever squeezed a person in my entire life.

"Be careful, *pocha* . . . you'll crush the baby."

"*Dios mío!*" Abuelita suddenly shouted.

I looked out into the evening rain. Stumbling up to the porch was Rodrigo. One eye was as big as a softball, his lip was split with a gigantic gash, and his shirt was torn and covered in blood.

"What happened?" I yelled as Rodrigo collapsed onto the front porch. But there was no need for me to ask, because the answer was obvious.

Locals, they don't like *pochos* messing with their women.

Abuelita went to the back of the house and got out her basket of medicine.

"This will hurt," she told my brother as she took out a jar of plants that had no name.

"My nose, Abuelita," Rodrigo complained. "I think they broke my nose."

Abuelita paused, looked at Rodrigo's nose, then reached out and yanked.

"Aaaargghh!" A gush of blood poured from his left nostril.

"There, it's fixed," Abuelita said. A moment later she reached under my brother's shirt and felt around his ribs. "You will urinate blood for a week, but you're lucky."

"Lucky? How'm I lucky?" my brother asked, in great pain.

Abuelita raised her head and looked at my brother with eyes that seemed to glow.

"You're lucky you're not dead."

The porch fell silent. We all knew she was right.

The next day Rodrigo complained that he was in too much pain to fly, but Abuelita told him it was his fault he had gotten into this mess and he had to take the flight.

"I can't, Abuelita," he said.

"You will," she said as the ranchero pulled up to

the property, and that ended the conversation. When Abuelita spoke in that tone of voice, everyone knew there was no arguing with her. Rodrigo limped toward the front seat of the truck and opened the door.

"In the back," she said.

Rodrigo looked up. Abuelita stared at him with a look that could have burned a hole through iron.

"I said, in the back," she repeated. "The ride in the front seat belongs to *tortuguita*."

"*¿Tortu . . . quién?*" Rodrigo asked with a puzzled look.

"*Tortuguita*," repeated my grandmother. She turned to me. "You have great strength, Sonia. Go . . . and do what you must."

A tear came to my eye. Abuelita reached out and hugged me. Her skin was soft and warm, quite unlike what I had expected.

"*Te quiero, Abuelita. Y muchas gracias.*"

"Listen to your heart, *tortuguita*. It's not the turtle's shell that protects it. It's the turtle's wisdom."

Tears dropped from my eyes when I told my grandmother I loved her. Then more tears came as I kissed the baby and hugged Maria good-bye. The baby smiled the whole time. My heart sank. While here, I felt I could protect Isabella, but with me in America, well, what would they do?

"E-mail me, *pocha*," said Maria.

"I will," I answered. "I will."

We hugged again.

The ranchero tossed our bags in the back of the truck, and Rodrigo climbed into the rear, his pain obvious.

"And you," said my grandmother to Rodrigo. "For you, I have only one piece of advice.

"What's that?" said my brother with a bitter look on his face. The hard surface of the truck and all the bouncing on unpaved roads would most certainly not make it a comfortable three-hour journey for him.

"Don't kiss the dog," said Abuelita. And just like that, the dirty mutt appeared from behind an old tractor tire. "Don't kiss the dog."

I smiled and closed the door. Eight weeks had gone by in the blink of an eye. I waved one last good-bye to Maria and Isabella and Abuelita, and we pulled away. For sure, I'd one day return to visit my grandmother's house, but a part of me knew it would never be like this again.

Never.

Before I knew it, the ranchero had gotten us to the airport, we'd crossed through security and were boarding our plane. I went to row twenty-two, seat B.

"That fucking dog," Rodrigo moaned. "All he did was lick his balls the whole trip."

Though originally I had been assigned to the window seat, I decided to give it to my brother. His lip was like a balloon, he couldn't lift his left arm, and I could tell from the way he wore his baseball cap low over his eyes that he had the kind of headache that made a person wish someone would just chop their head off. The least I could do was not make him sit in the middle seat for the whole flight.

I buckled my seat belt and tried to get comfortable.

"Can I offer you something to drink?" asked the stewardess after the plane took off.

"A Diet Coke, *por favor*," I said.

"And you, sir?" she asked my brother.

He answered without looking up. "Rum and coke, extra ice."

The stewardess paused. "Do you have ID?"

"*¿Qué?*" Rodrigo said.

"ID," she repeated. "You know, proof that you are of legal drinking age."

My brother paused.

"Okay, just give me *una cerveza*," said Rodrigo, in no mood to hear any back talk from her.

She paused. "Maybe you'd prefer a Diet Coke as well, sir?" she finally said.

"No, I'd prefer a beer," said Rodrigo.

"I'm sorry, but no ID, no alcohol."

"*Puta*," said Rodrigo under his breath, loud enough for her to hear.

The stewardess stared at my brother for a minute, debating what to do. Oh no, I thought, is she going to kick him off the plane? Have him arrested for being disorderly? Make us both stay in Mexico for a few more days until we work things out with the authorities. A person could get into a lot of trouble for mouthing off to airline people these days, and I had school on Monday.

However, the stewardess did none of those things. Instead, she just smiled.

"Enjoy your flight, sir. And if I can offer you anything nonalcoholic to drink, please let me know. It'd be my pleasure." The stewardess said it with such niceness that her message was crystal clear. In her eyes, Rodrigo was nothing more than a pathetic piece of crap, and she was not going to stoop to his level.

A few minutes later she handed me a Diet Coke. I reached into my wallet and gave her a two dollar tip.

"Thank you," I said.

"Are you sure you wouldn't like a refreshing nonalcoholic drink, sir? It's really quite delicious." She was teasing him.

"Pfft," said my brother. When she walked away, Rodrigo turned to me and asked, "Why you tippin' her?"

I paused, then took a sip of my Diet Coke. "For good service," I said. "After all, I don't want to be a lame-o."

I smiled. My brother grunted, lowered his baseball cap, and tried to sleep. After eight weeks in Mexico, Rodrigo was returning to the United States beaten up, broken down, and worn out. Me, I felt revitalized and refreshed, and as the plane zoomed skyward, I thought about how classes were starting again in a few days, and it was going to be my best year yet.

I had been wrong about Mexico. Totally wrong. And thank goodness.

What an amazing country.

chapter veíntítrés

I'd never been more excited to kick butt in school in my entire life. I didn't care what assignments were going to be thrown at me, what essay questions were going to be asked of me, or what stupid geometrical figures were going to be diagrammed for me in an attempt to make my brain spin, loop, bend, and twirl. History papers, chemistry problems, expository research assignments for English in MLA format . . . bring it on! I was so jazzed up that on the first day of junior year I went to the counselor's office and changed my entire schedule.

To AP classes.

"You sure you can handle this kind of workload?" the counselor asked with a skeptical look. "Five advance placement classes and computer graphics is going to be a heck of a lot of work."

I looked up with a glow in my eyes, a glow that had somehow come to me from Abuelita. "Bring it on," I said. The counselor saw my fire, nodded his head, and began tapping at his keyboard. In eighteen seconds my entire class schedule was changed. I was ready for anything.

Except what actually came.

For the first few weeks I was home, my mom was a giant pain in the rear. I heard *"Sonia . . . ayúdame,"* more than I'd ever heard in the prior sixteen years of my life. And my drunkle had pretty much dug himself in like a smelly vagrant who was never going to leave. All he did was drink, lose money gambling on the card game *Con Quian*, and make a total mess of *la casa*, with the expectation that I'd not only clean up after him but cook him hot meals along the way.

There was a bit of good news, though. Papi got a promotion and was earning two more dollars an hour at the gym. I was so proud when I heard about his pay raise. I knew he had earned it. But *mi papi*'s promotion meant more responsibility, and sometimes he worked even later into the night. Though I was slammed with things to do like never before, I was also inspired by his example of how hard work always paid off. So I did everything I could to attend to my schoolwork, homework, housework, and all my other chores.

And for a while I was pulling it off. Then my mother was put on bed rest, doctor's orders. Basically, the problem was she was too fat. I mean, it ain't like Mexican food is the healthiest anyway, and *mi ama* seemed to love cheese nowadays more than a mouse. She was eating whole blocks of the stuff at a time. Her ankles were swollen like inflatable tubes.

"For the twins," she would say in Spanish as she gobbled *queso Chihuahua*, a yellow cheese that was her favorite of them all. Between *mi ama* and Tía Luna, they were so fat, I thought it was only a matter of time before one of them sat and broke a chair.

Of course, *mi ama* had never been what I would call helpful when it came to making our home functional in the first place, but once she was ordered to do nothing but sit in her bed and watch *telenovelas* all day (oh, the tragedy), she became like a hospital patient. And I became the nurse. I even had to wash *mi ama's* underarms in the bathtub because she couldn't reach around her enormous *tetas* to get to her armpits.

Night after night I stayed up until one a.m., struggling to get all my homework done, and every morning my alarm clock would go off at 5:07, like some kind of cruel torture buzzer. For months I survived on four hours of sleep a night, and still, though I'd never worked harder to keep up, I barely pulled a C average for the first semester. Those AP classes were brutal and my duties around the house never ended, no matter how much I did. The positive vibes and momentum from my trip to Mexico were all but a dream when the new year came.

"Dang, where you been, girl?" Tee-Ay said to me one day when she saw me in the hall, second semester.

"I know," I answered. "I've been missing a ton of school." I lowered my eyes and looked at the ground in shame. There was no reason for me to even bother trying to explain what had been going on. Tee-Ay knew the reason.

Familia.

Truthfully, I expected Tee to rain down disapproval and hit me with more of that "You gotta do for you" stuff, but instead, she surprised me. Tee didn't want to fight. I guess she felt like I did—sorta sad that our lunchtime ritual was over and that we hardly saw each other anymore. I also got the sense that she wanted to talk, to chat with a friend. A real friend, the kind you can tell stuff to that you can't tell to other people. I looked into Tee-Ay's eyes and felt bad. I mean, what kind of person was I that couldn't even stay in touch with one of my closest peeps on the planet anymore? I could see she needed me, and I hadn't been there for her.

You're bad, Sonia, I thought. A really bad friend.

"Wanna share some fries?" Tee-Ay asked me.

I smiled.

"I would love to share some fries," I replied.

"I'll get the chips and sodas," Tee-Ay answered, her face lighting up.

"I'll get the fries," I added eagerly, hoping that the cafeteria ladies had cooked them real well-done that day. Maybe our lunchtime ritual was about to be rekindled. We each took off in separate directions without even bothering to talk about where we'd meet back up. That's because we both knew exactly where we'd meet: by the flagpole, in front of the library, at the third table to the left of the fence.

But like everything else in my life, things turned out different than I had planned. Violently different.

I never even saw it coming. All I felt was the hot pain searing through my skull. Blood flowed from my nose as if I had been smashed in the face with a hammer. My T-shirt was soaked in red liquid, my shoe fell off when I hit the ground, and the next day, I needed Tee-Ay to tell me what had happened, because after I got hit, I kinda blanked out.

I knew that it was Black History Month. The school had planned some special events and the day's schedule had been changed so that we had an extended second period. This meant that for the first part of second period, half the school went to an MLK Day assembly in the auditorium while the other half went to class.

Then everybody was supposed to switch. Half the school was supposed to go to the auditorium while the first group went to class.

However, as Tee-Ay explained, "supposed to" and "did" are two different things on our campus. About a hundred million kids ditched class and went to both assemblies. It was chaos.

And then it was lunch. After lunch, we were all supposed to go to third period and finish out the rest of the day as usual.

Once again, this is what we were "supposed to" do. It's not what happened.

During the second MLK assembly, which was packed with about a thousand more students than there should have been, some Latinos were goofing off during the performance and some blacks took it as "disrespect to their culture."

A fight broke out. It turned into a five-on-five brawl. Then lunch started, and the next thing everyone knew, students were dividing up all over campus, throwing punches at one another for no reason other than the color of their skin.

Hispanics and blacks fought, while Samoans and Filipinos gathered their own and tried to stay uninvolved.

Kids were getting jumped left and right.

Of course, Tee-Ay and I had no idea any of this was happening when we'd planned to share french fries. When we made our plan, we'd had no idea that the whole campus was already out of control, seized by violence.

Security had broken up the first few fights, but the action had spread to other areas around the school—by the band room, behind the gym, in the science corridor. Troublemakers cruised the campus like packs of wolves, attacking smaller groups of students who weren't with members of their own race to protect them. There just wasn't enough security to contain all the fighters.

BAM! Tee-Ay told me how three black kids stomped a Hispanic near a garbage can.

POP! She explained how four Latinos caught a baseball player and hit him in the kidneys with a bat.

WHHHOOOOSSHH! Someone set a fire in a trash can.

HMMVVVZZZ!!!!!! HMMVVVZZZ!!!!!!
The school bell sounded.

"As if a bell was going to make all the students stop rioting," Tee-Ay told me on the phone later. "It was teenage anarchy."

As I said, the only thing I experienced of the race riot was fiery pain shooting through my brain. Once I got hit, I immediately fell to the ground, and from there, everything went fuzzy. Someone told Tee that it was all an accident, that a big Latino guy was running away from a group of black kids, and as he raced by, I turned the corner to buy some french fries, and he accidentally nailed me with an elbow to the nose. Though I never saw what hit me, some people got me to the nurse's office, and then a neighbor came and gave me a ride to the emergency room.

I waited almost five hours for less than five minutes' worth of medical attention. What a surprise: brown-skinned people aren't getting the best health care in the United States. After all that time in the waiting room, they told me there was pretty much nothing they could do.

"Your nose isn't broken, here's some aspirin for the headache you're about to have, and don't worry when your eyes turn black and blue . . . because they will." That was it for my treatment. No compassion. No tenderness. Not even a real doctor; it was a male nurse who treated me.

As we left the emergency room, I noticed there were at least fifty more patients waiting, bleeding, suffering, desperate to see a doctor. And none of these people were white folks either. Coincidence? I don't think so.

"I look like a Mexican raccoon," I told Tee-Ay over the phone.

"I'm sure you don't," she said, trying to sound cheerful. "Well, maybe . . . but the cute kind, like a stuffed animal."

I laughed, but smiling hurt my face. The circles under my eyes were a combination of purple, black, and blue, and my nose was sore, like I had been in a fifteen-round boxing match with a rhinoceros. I hung up with Tee-Ay, rubbed my temples, and felt major thumping going on in my cranium.

No matter how much I had to do around the *casa*, what I really needed was to lie down and get a bit of rest. At first I fought the desire to nap, and began gathering up some laundry, but when I bent over I felt dizzy, so I dropped the pile of clothes and went to the kitchen to take a few more aspirin. When I entered *la cocina*, I found Tía Luna eating some *pollo asado*, roasted chicken. There was a shine of chicken grease around her mouth, and her fingers were slippery from sucking on the bones to get all the good meat out.

"*Dios mío,*" she said. "You look like a child of *El Diablo. ¿Qué pasa?*"

I shook my head. With the way my brain was pounding I couldn't deal with my stupid fat aunt's stupid fat comments. I opened the bottle of aspirin and poured myself some *agua.*

"You ignore me?" she said.

"I got hit in the face at school, okay?" I answered. "There was a race riot."

"Ah, the niggers," she responded in *español.* "They love to cause trouble. Children of the devil, all of them."

I glared at her.

"Don't you give me the evil eye," she said. "Especially when I speak the truth."

She slurped on the bone of a wing.

"Why do you hate me?" I asked.

She paused.

"Really, why do you hate me?" I said again.

"Jesus teaches us not to hate, Sonia, so I don't," Tía Luna answered. "But you, *mija,* are the worst kind of Mexican there is."

My aunt set down her chicken bones and reached for a cheapie paper towel.

"I mean, look at you. *Busca.* You turn your back on your culture, you disrespect your elders, and you

211

have no moral strength. All you care about is you. Pfft. You're an embarrassment to me and my kind, to real Mexican women."

She looked at me with loathing. "You are an embarrassment to our people." Tía Luna rolled up her paper towel and threw it in the garbage. "I'll pray for you, Sonia," she said, exiting the kitchen. "I will pray. But the devil is going to take you. You're doomed." A moment later, she left.

I stood there totally and completely stunned. Suddenly I started feeling nauseous. Then came the claustrophobia. If I didn't get out of the house immediately, I was going to puke.

"*Sonia . . .*" came a voice. "*Ayúdame!*"

I grabbed my jacket and raced for the door.

"*Sonia . . .*"

I flew past Tía Luna, stepped outside, and let the cool air hit me in the face. It felt like I was suffocating. *Breathe, Sonia. Breathe*, I told myself.

After a minute, I caught my breath. And then I started walking.

Away.

chapter veinticuatro

I wandered the streets. I had nowhere to go, no *dinero* in my pocket, no place to be, and no one who understood. Though America is filled with millions of people, it's also one of the loneliest places on earth. My feet moved along the sidewalks, but I had no idea where I was heading. I just walked.

I thought about killing myself. Seriously. Then I realized I didn't know how to do such a thing. I'd need rope. Or a bridge to jump off. Or maybe razor blades. All I knew was that I wanted to die. Really die. I had been walking and walking for hours when suddenly I looked up, not knowing where I was.

Santiago's Pet Store.

Impossible, I thought. How could such a thing happen? My heart was so heavy, I felt like I was wearing a wet sweater I couldn't take off.

I turned and gazed in the front window, but instead of seeing kittens, I saw rabbits. Some were white, others were brown. One looked light pink. My sadness grew. I decided to keep walking.

But I couldn't.

Despite the fact that I didn't believe in all that mumbo jumbo, I-was-pulled-there stuff, it seemed that I had no choice but to go inside. Why? Because somehow, some way, I had been pulled there.

But I couldn't go in, I told myself.

Yet I had to.

Mi cabeza screamed at my legs to "run away," but *mi corazón*—not screaming, but quiet like a whisper—told my body to "stay and enter." And in the battle of heart and mind, heart always seems to win.

I opened the door and heard the jingle of the little bell. I was entering, raccoon eyes and all.

It took a few moments, but soon I heard his voice.

"Goodness, a long summer trip this was," he said. Then there was a pause. "But it seems that only the rings under your eyes got a tan."

Geraldo smiled. Seeing the gentle look in his eyes made me instantly start to tear up. He gently brushed the hair from my face.

"Your sadness has such beauty," he said. "But you

do know your true nature is like that of rainbows and butterflies, don't you?"

I didn't answer.

"I missed you deeply, Sonia." He brushed back another piece of my hair and smiled with perfect, white teeth. "But now, well . . . you are back."

"Weren't you worried I'd never return?" I asked.

"Of course not," he said with confidence. "Remember? It is written."

I took a deep breath, the kind that stutters when you try to fill your lungs with air because of all the tears you've been crying. But the heaviness of the wet sweater on my heart was starting to lift.

"Wait," Geraldo suddenly said. "I think there is someone else who would like to see you."

"Frijolito," I called out, unable to contain my joy when he returned with the cat. "*Dios mío*, look how you've grown." I started scratching behind the kitten's left ear, the one with the muscle that wasn't strong enough to make it stand all the way up. Frijolito immediately started to purr.

"Your phone number still works?" Geraldo asked.

"Don't call," I said.

"But you came," he answered.

Suddenly the fuzziness started to clear, and I began to remember where I was and how I had gotten here.

"I made a mistake," I answered, handing him back the cat.

"Maybe you didn't," Geraldo said, holding Frijolito in his arms.

"No," I said. "I did. *Lo siento*, Geraldo. I'm sorry. I really am."

I left without another word.

chapter veinticinco

Of course I returned home. And of course, when I did, no one asked me how I was feeling. They only wanted to know what the dinner plans were. I told them we'd be having KFC, and I wrote down the order on a piece of paper. Then I asked Rodrigo to go pick it up. There was a *fútbol* game on TV and he said no. I asked my younger brother Oscar to go. He sat on the couch right next to Rigo and told me no in the exact same tone of voice. Then, instead of just asking my brother Miguel, I changed my strategy and made him an offer of bribery. He was my last chance.

"I'll give you extra money for *nieve de fresa*, which you can eat before dinner if you do this for me."

"A double scoop," he counteroffered.

"Okay," I said. Really, I couldn't have given a damn if he ate a whole bucket of ice cream; all I wanted was to survive the evening.

Which I did.

The next day my headache pounded a lot less, and I decided not to think about anything and just focus on working. There was so much to do. The floors needed washing, the shower needed cleaning, and the bedsheets needed changing. Call me a freak, but there is nothing like a few loads of laundry to make problems disappear. I even sent Maria an e-mail.

Hola, Prima,
    Things at home are just GR8T. Better than ever.
    I'm kicking butt in school, and my love life is absolutely purr-fect.
    Juicy details soon. I miss the porch.
Amor to you & Abuelita & (most important) my little angel, Isabella.
xoxoxo,
Pocha

Wow, I never realized how easy it was to lie.

Later that evening, when I went to take out the garbage, which of course none of my brothers ever did, someone popped out from behind the Dumpster, scaring me half to death.

"Ah!" I said, jumping back.

"Whoa, didn't mean to startle you."

"Geraldo? You followed me?"

"Technically, I think I stalked you."

I looked over my shoulder to see if my drunkle could see me out the back door. "You must go. You can't be here."

"But who will I give this to?" he asked.

Slowly Geraldo reached into his jacket and pulled out the kitten.

"Awww, Frijolito," I said. "But I can't have a cat."

"Too bad," he answered as he passed Frijolito to me. "You do."

"But I can't," I repeated as I took him in my arms. According to superstition, cats and babies are like oil and water, and *mi ama* was due to give birth any day now. There was no way she would allow it.

"The store just got a new dog."

"A dog?" I said with fear.

"A mean one. The kind that doesn't like cats," he said. I nervously bit my lower lip. "His name is . . ." Geraldo paused for dramatic effect. *"Dientes."*

"Uh," I said in shock. The dog's name was *Teeth*.

"You see, this is why I brought him to you," Geraldo told me. "It was either here or *la calle*."

"The streets?"

"We're a pet store, not a pet hotel, and no one

wants a lumpy cat," he said with a shrug of his shoulders. "I mean, no one but you."

I stroked Frijolito behind the ear in his favorite spot, and he began to purr. Quickly, I looked over my shoulder to see if anyone was watching, and thought of a plan.

The garage.

I could hide some food and milk, maybe a bed. It wouldn't be perfect, and I'd have to make sure I sneaked out there without anyone noticing, but I thought I could pull it off.

"Sonia . . ." a voice suddenly called out. It was my drunkle. Luckily, I was wearing an oversized hoodie sweatshirt. I quickly tucked Frijolito inside next to my stomach.

"*Estoy aquí, Tío,*" I called out. Then I turned to Geraldo. "You must go."

"Have lunch with me."

"Go."

"Dinner."

"Go, Geraldo, I am serious. *Vete!*"

"Breakfast, snacks, a midafternoon cup of tea."

I pushed him away. "Leave, Geraldo. Go. You MUST stay away."

Finally, Geraldo started walking away, slowly stepping backward down the alley.

"It is written, Sonia. Remember, we are written."

Geraldo bowed, turned, then made a right at the corner as my drunkle stepped outside. *Mi tío* looked down the alley just as Geraldo disappeared.

"*¿Quién es?*" he asked.

"*Nadie,*" I answered softly.

My drunkle wrinkled his brow and stared far off into the distance.

"Hmm, *un cerote*," he said. "They can smell your pussy from a mile away." He continued to look down the alley for the boy who was no longer there, then commanded to me in Spanish. "Centrals are foul people, Sonia. Stay away."

I lowered my eyes and looked at the ground, hoping my drunkle wouldn't see the big lump I was desperately trying to hide in the belly of my sweatshirt. Thankfully, Frijolito lay against my stomach perfectly still.

"Dinner will be ready in twenty-five minutes," I answered, not looking up.

My drunkle stared at me for a moment then, satisfied his words would be obeyed like the orders of a king, he turned and walked back into the house.

I headed for the garage to make accommodations for my new cat. Jesucristo, was my family racist.

Cerote is like a curse word used for Salvadorans

by Mexicans. Of course, white folks and black people think all brown-skinned people are the same, but we're not. In fact, in the Hispanic community, there's a lot of ethnic stuff going on. All Latinos are NOT the same, and all Latinos are NOT Mexican, and *cerote* and *Central* are very bad, offensive words. Salvadorans return the insult when they call us *wetbacks* or *beaners*. It's funny how so many brown people say they are the victims of racism in the United States, and yet they are just as racist themselves.

I laid down an old blanket for Frijolito in the back corner of the garage, not believing that my drunkle had had the nerve to tell me I couldn't see Geraldo. I mean, didn't he know that when you tell a teenage girl she can't date a boy, the first thing it makes her want to do is go out and date that boy?

What an *idiota*.

The next day, I went to the pet store.

"I knew you'd come," he said with a smile.

"You didn't know," I answered.

"I knew," he said.

"Well, I'm only here for toys."

"Uh-huh."

"And food."

"Uh-huh.

"And bowls. A kitten needs to have good bowls."

I wandered through the aisles, looking over the various types of items that were sold. "In your professional opinion, are these good bowls?"

Geraldo stepped so close I could feel his heat.

"Have dinner with me?"

"I don't think . . ."

"Lunch?"

"I . . ."

"Breakfast?

"What, a Snickers bar?" I said with a laugh.

"I was thinking eggs . . . after we stay up all night talking, looking deeply into one another's eyes, and telling small jokes that make us giggle and hug and want to watch the orange sunrise together."

My heart skipped a beat.

"When?" I asked.

"Now."

"I can't now."

"Then later."

"When later?"

"Whenever," he replied. "If it takes a thousand years, I already know, for you I will wait."

His passion was undeniable. How could I say no? We made a plan to have lunch in two days.

chapter veintiséis

I had to take the bus for more than an hour to get to where Geraldo wanted to meet for lunch, but I was glad to make the long trip. This way, there was no chance of running into anyone I knew, and word getting back to *mi familia* about the boy from El Salvador with emerald green eyes.

He chose a place called Pupusería Suchitotal, a traditional Salvadoran restaurant.

"Do you like the *pupusas*?" he asked before I could even finish chewing the first bite. I could tell by the way he inquired that he was eagerly hoping I'd say yes.

"*Sí,*" I answered. "They are delicious."

"They are made exactly like they make them in my family's home town of Suchitoto. There's corn meal, spices, beans, and cheese," he said, taking great pride in explaining the ingredients to me. "And that is *curtido*," he said, pointing to the other food on my plate. "It's kind of a cabbage salad with vinegar."

"It's all really good," I said after taking another bite. I could tell Geraldo was pleased. Like all Latinos, traditional foods are a big part of his culture and I knew he must have been worried that if I didn't like the *pupusas*, there was probably no way I was going to like him.

"Suchitoto, is that your hometown?" I asked.

"No," he answered. "I was born here. My family had to flee during the civil war."

"Oh," I said. Though Geraldo didn't come right out and say it, I could tell by his tone that his parents were illegals, too. Us Latinos have a way of saying things to one another without exactly saying them.

"Have you ever been?" he asked.

"Me," I answered with a laugh. Like my family would ever approve of me taking a trip to El Salvador. "Uhm, no."

"It's a small town," he said as he took another bite of his food. "You can see the hills, feel the wind against your face, smell fresh air." Geraldo looked out at the busy, traffic-filled streets of Los Angeles. "I like it there very much. *Es tranquilo*. Very calm."

"Do you want to go back one day?" I asked.

He paused before answering.

"My family hopes I will one day return," he said. "But I'm an American. At least, a Hispanic American, or a Salvadoran American, or a Chicano American, some type of hyphen person. Sometimes I kind of feel like a human being between two worlds, you know, like one of my feet is on a boat and the other is on a dock, and I can't step on to either side; I'm just caught in the middle. Does that make any sense to you?" he asked.

"More than you know," I replied.

"I think my parents, when they look at me, they are afraid they are going to lose their culture, so they ask lots of unrealistic things of me," he said. "It's like, because they don't speak any English, sometimes it feels as if they are the child and I am the parent."

Geraldo noticed that my soda was down to the halfway point in my cup, so, with the grace of a true gentleman, he stood to refill my drink.

"*Con permiso,*" he said, reaching over to take my glass. A moment later he came back with a Coca-Cola filled to the tippy-top.

"*Gracias,*" I said.

"*De nada,*" he replied as he sat back down.

"You know, America is my home, but sometimes I don't really feel like I have anyone I can speak with." He paused. "Up until now, that is. For some reason, it's easy for me to talk to you."

He looked at me with those gorgeous green eyes. I lowered my gaze and quietly took another bite of food.

"My family lost everything in the war," he continued. "But one day, I am determined to make it in America and restore pride to my family name. But I'm not going to do it the wrong way," he insisted. "I will do it properly, with brains and hard work, not drugs and crime. I guess you could say I am a *tradicionalista*."

"A *tradicionalista*?" I asked. "And what exactly does that mean?" I said, curious to know what his idea of a traditionalist was.

"For one, it means no sex before marriage," he answered.

My eyes got big.

"But," he continued, "I have to admit, when I get close to you I have very deep desires to know your flesh."

I flushed with heat.

There was no way I could date Geraldo. I had too much work, too many problems, I needed to get school back up and rolling, and *mi familia* would never, ever approve.

But I had never felt this way about a boy in my entire life. Geraldo leaned across the table and kissed me. It was tender yet sensual. My heart exploded.

We began to date in secrecy.

chapter veintisiete

As I rode the bus back home that afternoon, I wondered if this was how my cousin Maria had felt about Juan Carlos when she'd first started to see him. My whole body tingled, and for *el primero* time in my life, I knew I was head over heels in love. Nothing could ever stop us.

Geraldo began showing up at my house after his shift at the pet store, before he went to his evening classes. He was studying business at night school with a plan to become an Internet entrepreneur one day. Geraldo swore there was a giant international market still to be tapped by better connecting Mexico and Central America to the emerging power of China, with the expertise of American engineers. Truthfully, I wasn't sure I understood all of his big ideas about multinational businesses, but Geraldo was passionate, intelligent, and determined. I had no doubt that one day he'd be an amazing success. We started meeting at prearranged times behind the Dumpster in the back alley when I'd take out the garbage.

"Stalker," I said as I fell into his arms and kissed him.

"I must see you more," he pleaded.

"We can't see each other more," I said, kissing him again.

"We must," he insisted.

"I keep throwing perfectly fine things out just to make more garbage," I said with a laugh. "I think our relationship is bad for the environment."

"You're right, we should recycle," he answered. "We'll start with a recycled kiss. This is like the one I gave you yesterday," he said as his lips tickled my neck. "This is like the one I gave you a few minutes ago," he continued as I smiled with a heart full of joy. "And this is like the one I am going to give you on May fifth."

"*Alto,*" I said, telling him to stop but praying that he never, ever would. "But why May fifth?" I asked between kisses.

"Because that is my birthday," he answered. "And your lips will be my present."

"Consider it a deal," I answered as he leaned in again. "*Te lo prometo.* I promise."

Then we heard a noise. A moment later, my

brother Rodrigo stumbled out from behind a Dumpster about fifteen yards away. He exhaled a big cloud of smoke. Obviously he was smoking pot.

Then, right behind him, followed my drunkle. He was coughing. *Dios mío*, Rodrigo and my drunkle were smoking *mota* together.

They looked up and were just as surprised to see Geraldo and me as we were to see them. Rodrigo moved first. He walked right past us into the house without saying a word. My drunkle, however, stayed where he was and looked Geraldo up and down. There was menace in his eye. A second later, he started to approach.

Geraldo straightened up tall, as if he wanted to clear up something with my drunkle, even though I had never dared mention anything to him too personal about *mi tío*. But I had spent a good deal of time talking about how unfairly I was treated by most of *mi familia*—okay, especially by my drunkle—and now I was regretting every bad word I'd ever said. I sensed trouble.

Big trouble.

"Geraldo, go," I said.

"No, there's a few things I'd like to clarify with this gentleman."

"No, Geraldo, you mustn't," I said, holding him

back. "Please." My drunkle was heading straight toward us. "Please, Geraldo, go," I repeated. "For me."

Geraldo lowered his eyes from my drunkle and looked down at my pleading face.

"Violence will not solve anything," I said. "I beg you, do not stoop to this level."

Geraldo paused and considered my words.

"Out of respect for you," he said, and began to walk away.

My drunkle glared with a machismo stare at Geraldo. "*Vámonos,*" he said, ordering me inside.

I didn't move.

"*Te dije, vámonos,*" he repeated with more authority. I could tell my drunkle wasn't going to say it a third time. Not wanting him to grab me by the arm and drag me into the house, I began walking inside. If Geraldo would have seen my drunkle touch me, I am sure he would have come running back.

I headed indoors. Suddenly I heard a screech.

"*Vete!*" my drunkle said.

"*Meow!*"

I spun my head around and saw Frijolito scampering away.

Bastard! I thought. What kind of scumbag kicks a cat?

"*Vé,*" he commanded to me again. We walked through the back door.

Once inside, we found *mi ama* out of bed and on the couch, sitting with Tía Luna, Rodrigo, and two of my younger brothers.

"I needed some air," *mi ama* said in defense of not being in bed like the doctor had ordered. She was plump as a moose.

I expected there to be mutual silence between me and my drunkle. I wouldn't say anything about the fact that he had been out back smoking pot with my brother, and he wouldn't say anything about Geraldo.

"Your daughter is fooling around with a *cerote,*" he said, loud enough for everyone to hear.

Tía Luna and *mi ama* looked up at me in total shock. My jaw dropped. Before I could think of what to say in response, or calculate what the consequences would be for my words if I did say them, my drunkle added more fuel to the fire.

"Since her father has to work so much, it's easy for a girl to get into trouble."

I just stood there like an idiot . . . stupid, silent, and stunned as he snitched on me. *Mi ama* and Tía Luna started nodding their heads up and down in agreement like those silly little bobble-head dolls.

"I told her, you can't trust Centrals."

"It's true, you can't trust Centrals, Sonia," said Tía Luna, warning me not to see this boy anymore. "Inside the dark skin is where the devil does his best work." My aunt reached over and started rubbing the twins in *mi ama's* tummy. "Let us pray for light skin."

A sad truth about Mexican families is that the more light-skinned a baby is, the better it is treated in some homes. Lighter-skinned children get more positive attention, are given more opportunities, and often have an easier time in life. When a child is brown in the Latino community, being too brown is not a good thing.

I stood there amazed by the fact that my drunkle was scoring major brownie points with *mi ama* and Tía Luna for ratting me out about Geraldo and being considered a great family member when five minutes earlier he had just been outside getting stoned with my teenage brother.

"*Gracias*, Ernesto," said *mi ama*. "It's hard to keep an eye on your kids in El Norte."

"You don't have to thank me," said my drunkle as he went to the refrigerator and opened a beer. "*Somos familia*. We are family."

I glared at my drunkle with nothing but hate. Tía Luna saw the look in my eyes and disapprovingly shook her head.

"And when your *madre* is at this point in her pregnancy, you bring this into the *casa*," she said as everyone stared at me. "Pfft . . . Maybe you should just go and start dinner."

"*Sí, Sonia,*" said *mi ama*, nodding her head in agreement. "Go."

That evening the moon was full. And it was hot out. Usually, California sees the temperature get cool in the nighttime, but since Los Angeles is pretty much located in a desert, sometimes the weather stays really warm.

We turned every fan in our house to high. Still, we were all uncomfortable.

At about 11:45 p.m I was sitting at my study table in a T-shirt and pajama pants, trying, however pathetically, to get a bit of schoolwork done. Tackling chemistry problems while struggling to figure out all the elements of the periodic table when I had missed all kinds of important class lectures on science was as good a way as any to forget that I had just been told by my mother to never again see the love of my life.

I heard the sound of a key in the door.

"*¿Papi?*" I called out. Maybe he was getting home early.

"*Buenas,*" came a raspy voice. It was my drunkle. He almost never came home from the bars this early. I saw him stumble inside after pulling his key out of the door. The entire *casa* was asleep.

He smiled with red, bloodshot eyes and surveyed the room.

"*Tengo hambre,*" he commanded, informing me that he was hungry. "*Sonia, hazme comida.*"

I glared and paused, debating whether to cook for him or disobey. A moment later I threw down my pencil and stormed into the kitchen, figuring I'd quickly make him a *quesadilla* or something to get him off my back. I was too pissed off to be scared of him.

But I should have been.

"*Estás enojada,*" he said, telling me that he could see I was upset. But he said it with a smile. It was as if he found my anger attractive. I didn't answer.

"Don't be angry, *mija*, but you must understand, it's too easy to become an American whore."

Not being able to stand the sight him, I turned around and faced the stove. With my back to him, I lit the burner.

"The problem is, you are too proud," he said. "You forget who you are. Who your people are. Where you come from."

I placed a tortilla in the pan.

"It's good that I am here to watch over you. After all, Sonia . . . *somos familia.* We are family."

Suddenly I felt a hand reach under my shirt from behind and gently caress my breast.

My brothers were asleep, *mi ama* was in bed, and *mi papi* wasn't home from work yet. I froze.

His finger started to work its way around my nipple. There was no voice in my throat with which to scream. I just stood there with my feet feeling as if they were locked to the floor. Coldness ran through my blood.

"AAAAHHHHHHH!"

Suddenly, there was a scream.

"AAAAHHHHHHH!" came the cry again. *"¡ES TIEMPO!"*

We both turned. *Mi ama's* voice rang through the air like the shriek of an eagle. "It's time!" she cried out. "It's time!" Her water had just broke.

Suddenly lights flipped on, and my brothers were running from room to room, Tía Luna was called on the phone, and the whole house exploded to life.

Next thing I knew, we were off to the hospital. The twins were on their way.

chapter veintiocho

Mi ama needed a C-section to deliver the babies. There had been complications, and she had lost a lot of blood. Luckily, the twins were fine, but the quick look I got at *mi ama* after her surgical delivery told me she was in pretty bad shape. Her eyes were cloudy, and although she was medicated on all sorts of drugs, I could tell she was still in pain. I watched as they rolled her off to a recovery room while the babies were taken to the pediatric ward so they could be bathed, given some tests, and wrapped like mini-burritos in hospital blankets.

Mi papi missed the birth—after all, it wasn't *Navidad* number one or number two, and he had to finish his shift at the gym—but when he got to the hospital, the nurses let him hold the twins after he washed his hands. He held one new baby in each arm as if they were two big Easter baskets of special goodies from Jesus and Mary themselves. I'd never seen him smile so big in all my life.

Watching the happiness on *mi papi's* face made me realize that for him, more babies didn't represent more mouths to feed. Nor did they represent more burden he'd need to carry, more hours he'd need to work, or less free time of his own to sit on the couch and watch TV or do things like play golf (which Mexicans never did. The closest we came to golf courses was watering the grass.). To *mi papi*, more babies represented more love. Pure love. He literally beamed with pride.

"Aren't they beautiful, Sonia?" he asked.

"Sí, Papi," I said in a low voice. *"Sí."*

Mi papi looked me over.

"¿Qué pasa, mija?"

I debated telling him.

"Mija . . ." he asked again, seeing the concern on my face. *"¿Qué?"*

"I . . . I just . . ."

I didn't know how to say it. He waited patiently.

"Papi, did you smile like this when I was born?" I asked.

Papi paused. A moment later he turned the twins to the left while he rotated his head to the right to speak to me privately.

"Sshhh, don't tell this to the babies, because I

don't want them to get jealous or anything, but for you, my *tortuguita*, I smiled the most."

A tear came to my eye. *Mi papi* always knew the right thing to say.

"*Ahorita dígame, mija. ¿Qué pasa?*"

Again he asked me what was wrong.

"*Nada, Papi. Nada,*" I answered. "I'm just worried about Ama, that's all."

Despite the complications, *mi ama* had stabilized, but it was hours before we could see her. When we did, her eyes were all foggy, and I am not sure if she even knew we were in the room.

Mi ama's C-section had been a big surgery. However, in El Norte, a big surgery doesn't mean a big hospital stay. Not when you're an uninsured Mexican, it doen't.

Most C-sections require at least four days in the recovery ward. Some women stay for a week or even ten days. *Mi ama* was sent home after only two-and-a-half days because the county hospital needed the bed space.

"Yet she's still in pain," *mi papi* protested.

"There's nothing I can do."

"But you're the doctor."

"Doctors don't make these decisions anymore, Mr. Rodriguez. Administrators do."

El doctor began to scribble on a notepad. "Here's

a prescription," he said. "These pills are for pain."

My father looked up with deep concern in his eyes. The doctor looked back with sympathy. *"Lo siento, señor, pero mis manos están atadas,"* he answered. Then he turned to me and shrugged his shoulders. "My hands are. tied," he repeated, and walked off to attend to more patients.

A few hours later, after pages and pages of paperwork that I had to fill out and Papi had to sign, *mi ama* was discharged and sent home to bed rest, *telenovelas*, and little orange pills that were supposed to make the pain go away. Of course, I never did say anything to *mi papi* about my drunkle. I guess the opportunity never presented itself again. Besides, who had time for conversation? As the twins' baby nurse, I barely had time to pee. There were diapers to change, feedings to give, clothing to wash, bottles to rinse, late-night rockings, early-morning poops, and fits of crying that seemed to come out of nowhere and then stop for no reason at all. And since *mi ama* was trying to recuperate from major surgery, I had been turned into a human caregiving machine.

There were three of them, and only one of me, and I was getting my butt kicked like never before. If I got three hours' worth of sleep in a row, I was lucky. I had become a zombie.

Making matters worse, every male in *mi casa* was completely worthless except for *mi papi*, who had to return to work after missing only two days. After all, there's no such thing as a paternity leave for under-the-table towel washers in a sports club. Also, I was sure that Tía Luna was purposefully dragging her feet every time she tried to help just so I would have to work even harder. I wasn't able to shower, I missed every prearranged meeting time with Geraldo, and even though I had ten days off for spring break, when classes resumed after the holiday, I still could not make it to *escuela*. If I had been barely hanging on in school last semester, this semester I was entirely dropping the ball.

But what could be done?

"*Sonia . . .*" *mi ama* called out. I stared at another round of bottles that needed to be washed. Two weeks had passed since the twins had come home. "*Me duele,*" she cried out. "I am in pain."

She wanted her pills. I filled a glass with *agua*, unscrewed the childproof safety top off the medicine bottle, and removed two small super-powerful orange painkillers.

One for her, one for me.

chapter veintinueve

A few nights later I heard a rock at the window. My stomach fluttered. It had to be Geraldo. It had been over three weeks since I'd seen him, and I had not returned any of his phone calls. I'd been ignoring him.

Then I heard a second rock. Geraldo must have been outside looking at me through our cheap drapes while I had my study light on. I shook my head at the thought of it. My study light used to be for school; these days, the only time I used it was when I was folding baby laundry. How sad, I thought. I ignored the *tap-tap-tap* of the pebbles against the window, hoping Geraldo would get the message and just go away.

But of course he didn't. Instead, he moved up to throwing stones. When one crashed so loud that it almost broke the window, I knew it was just a matter of time before he heaved some kind of Fred

Flintstone-size boulder. It was no use ignoring him. Though I couldn't see out into the night, I turned, waved, and pointed to the back of the house. Like it or not, I was going to have to meet him behind the Dumpsters.

I guess I'd always known this moment would come. I stepped out back and took a deep breath. He leaned in for a kiss. I turned away.

"We cannot see each other," I said coldly.

"I don't understand."

"What's not to understand? Mexicans and Salvadorans don't mix. Stripes and plaids don't mix. Me and you, we don't mix."

"But where is this coming from?"

"Because I'm a stupid beaner and you're a stupid Central, and this whole stupid thing will never work, okay? You must leave, Geraldo."

"I won't."

"You must. Now."

"I love you."

"*Cállate!*" I snapped. "Shut up. Don't talk like that."

"But you know I love you, Sonia. You are my destiny."

I paused and looked back at the house of *mi familia*.

"But you are not mine," I replied. For the first

time ever, I saw that Geraldo's spirit had been wounded.

"*Hasta luego, Geraldo. Y buena suerte.* Good luck."

Without another word, I started inside.

"We were born to be together, Sonia. Born to be like the ink that writes the pages of a great love story. And nothing will ever tear us apart. Nothing, you hear?"

I closed the door behind me, turned the latch, and told myself I would never go out there to meet him again.

Never.

The truth is I would have thought saying good-bye to the love of my life would have hurt more than it did. I guess all the hurt from everything else had started to numb me.

Like six weeks later, when my report card informed me that I had earned F's in all five of my AP classes, and an F in Computer Graphics, too, I didn't get all emotional about it. I just made the only logical choice I could.

I dropped out of school at the start of senior year.

"Yes, I am here to check out," I said to the woman working in the front office. If I had expected anyone to care, my delusions were completely shattered when the secretary responded without even looking up from the notepad she was writing on.

"You need to see Mrs. Javellano," she replied with a point of her pencil down the hall.

I headed toward the office to meet a lady whose name I had never heard before. When I got to a door with a sign that had her name on it, I stopped and knocked.

"Yes," came a voice.

"Hi, I'm here to check out," I said.

A middle-aged Latina wearing a nice, colorful pantsuit and fashionably thin eyeglasses stopped what she was doing, paused, and looked at me with suspicion. "And your name is?" she asked as she waved me into her office and motioned for me to take a seat.

"Sonia," I answered. "Sonia Rodriguez. ID number 4046351." I told her that extra bit of info about my ID because there were probably at least five other girls named Sonia Rodriguez who attended this school.

"And why do you wish to drop out, Sonia?" she asked.

Like, why do you care? I thought. But I didn't say that. After all, there was no need to be rude.

"I just do," I answered.

Mrs. Javellano typed my information into her

computer and took a moment to look over my records. "AP classes, huh? And a history of good grades. Is there something going on, Sonia? Something you want to talk about?"

I looked down. "I just want to check out," I replied. I knew I was allowed to. I was old enough to not need my parents' permission. In fact, I didn't even have to notify the school. I could have just stopped coming, like other kids did, but I didn't want to create extra work for anybody. I might be a high-school dropout, but at least I'm a high-school dropout who took into consideration the feelings of other people.

"Have you thought about home studies?" Mrs. Javellano asked.

I rolled my eyes.

"I'm serious," she said.

"Isn't that a program for kids who are on probation from juvenile hall or girls who are pregnant?"

"So you're not pregnant?"

"No," I answered. And who was she to ask such a thing, anyway? She was just some paper pusher in an office no one ever visited. I glared at her, but she didn't take any offense. I guess I wasn't the type of person who had a really mean glare. Instead, she looked back at me with warm, chocolate-colored eyes.

"A lot of students choose home studies as an

option to graduate. I mean, who knows? Maybe one day you'll decide you want to go to community college or something."

I hesitated. *Community college?* She must have seen the spark in my eye.

"*Es verdad,*" she replied. "Look, *mija*, we have got to get more Latinas walking these halls with diplomas instead of babies."

"I told you, I'm not pregnant," I said.

"*Bueno,*" she answered. "Then do me a favor, try home studies. I don't know what it is," she said, "but I have a feeling about you. A good feeling."

I lowered my eyes and stared at the floor.

"Well, you shouldn't," I said.

"But I do," she answered. Mrs. Javellano then reached across her desk and handed me a packet. "Will you try?" she asked.

I didn't want to be rude, so I nodded my head yes.

On the way back to *mi casa*, I looked through the first series of worksheets Mrs. Javellano had given me and realized how simple the assignments would be. There was no challenge to the material at all. Everything was so easy. All I'd need was the time to sit down and actually fill in the answers.

But of course, I wouldn't get it.

chapter treinta

I arrived home to *mi ama* and Tía Luna, who were both in a state of panic. Apparently, my drunkle had been arrested by the *policía* for attempting to steal a car stereo out of a BMW.

Personally, I was glad to hear he was locked up, and I hoped they'd throw away the key. After all, this was the fourth time he'd been busted for the same type of crime. The last time it had happened was during my sophomore year, when it cost me six days of class and resulted in my getting into a huge fight about *familia* and personal responsibility with Tee-Ay. We ended our differences maturely, though.

I told her to *mét.elo en tu culo*, stick it up your ass.

I thought about my drunkle and shook my head. *¡Jesucristo, que estúpido!* I said to myself. Didn't he know about car alarms?

"Poor Ernesto," my aunt moaned as she contemplated the idea of my drunkle being locked behind bars. Thank goodness one of the twins started crying in the other room because I couldn't bear to listen to Tía Luna make any more excuses about how her brother was a victim of society and had been forced into a life of crime because racist white men were always keeping down the brown man in El Norte.

After a diaper change, I returned a few minutes later carrying Cecilia, my baby sister, in my arms.

"They are threatening him with jail and deportation," Tía Luna whined, still talking about it.

"*Pobrecito,*" replied *mi ama* with an up-and-down shake of her head.

Yeah, poor Uncle Ernesto, I thought. Really, I didn't see why they were so upset. As usual, *mi ama* would come to my drunkle's rescue by raiding all of *mi papi*'s savings to post bail, and then, as usual, in a matter of hours my drunkle would be set free by the courts, come home from jail, and be drinking at the bars right around the corner from our house before he had even taken a shower. All in all, he'd probably spend less than thirty-six hours in lockup.

Sure enough, the next day my drunkle returned to *mi casa* holding a pink citation requesting his appearance in court at a future date.

"America is so stupid," he said as he cracked a beer, slurped, and waved the pink citation in the air. "You think Mexico would ever do for them what they do for us? We have no health care, El Norte gives us doctors. We have no documents, El Norte lets us send our kids to their schools. We break the law, El Norte gives us colorful pieces of paper and a warning. Ooh, a warning, I am *soooo* scared."

My drunkle tore up the citation and tossed it into the air like confetti. *"Salud América,"* my drunkle said as he raised his beer in a toast. "To a country of *pendejos*!"

My younger brothers laughed. I shook my head. Yet another wonderful lesson for the next generation of Latinos.

"Like I'm gonna show up at some stupid court hearing," he continued. "After all, what's the worst America will do to me, give me another pink citation? Or a blue one? Hell, I'll collect the whole fucking rainbow."

"Ernesto . . ." said *mi ama* as a meek warning for my drunkle to watch his language. In response, my drunkle chuckled, raised his beer, and finished the bottle in two giant gulps. I couldn't watch anymore. *Mi tío* manifested every crappy stereotype *gabachos* held about Latinos, and here he was, sitting in the middle of our living room laughing about it. Truly, it nauseated me. But when I looked over at *mi ama* and Tía Luna I saw contented little smiles. They were just happy he was free. Our *familia* was together again. To them, that's all that mattered.

Suddenly my drunkle went to the hallway closet and grabbed *mi papi*'s most prized possession on this planet: his signed Roberto Clemente baseball bat. As soon as we saw what he was doing, everyone in the room got tense.

Roberto Clemente, in *mi papi's* opinion, was the greatest baseball player who had ever lived. I can't even remember how many times while we were growing up *mi papi* would go to the hallway closet, get his Roberto Clemente bat, and talk about how his favorite ballplayer had done so much for Hispanic people. How he had carried himself with style, poise, and grace in spite of all the racism he'd faced in the big leagues. Of course, a lot of people remember Clemente as the first Latin baseball player elected to the Hall of Fame, but that's not why *mi papi* owned this bat. *Mi papi* owned it because Roberto Clemente had died in a plane crash while trying to help other people; trying to deliver relief supplies for earthquake victims in Nicaragua. None of that "Central/beaner" stuff meant anything to *mi papi*. In his eyes, Roberto

Clemente was a true Hispanic hero, a man to be respected and idolized for his values, not just his sports accomplishments. Clemente had made the ultimate sacrifice for his people when he could have just chased girls and enjoyed the good life of wealth and fame. Now that was a man to look up to. A man who led by example.

Papi had bought this bat the month Clemente died, and it was, for as long as I could remember, absolutely off limits for anyone to touch. We all knew it. My drunkle knew it too.

But *mi papi* wasn't home. And my boozed-up drunkle, feeling cocky about how he was duping America, suddenly thought he was king of the world and started waving Papi's Roberto Clemente bat around like he was some kind of brown-skinned Babe Ruth, beer gut and all.

Even one scratch on this bat would have set my father off in a rage. Everyone watched with fear as my drunkle recklessly swung it in the house.

"*Ernesto, por favor,*" said *mi ama*, trying to convince him to put down the bat.

"Oh, Alfredo wouldn't mind. *Somos hermanos,*" my drunkle replied. "*Somos familia.*"

We are brothers? We are family? Is that what he just said? *Jesucristo*, what a joke! If *mi papi* was here,

I was positive my drunkle would have been singing a different tune.

But of course *mi papi* wasn't here. He was off doing what he had to do to support the needs of his *familia*. Like Roberto Clemente, *mi papi* showed our household how to live the proper way through actions, not words. That was how he always led us. Always by example.

After a few more minutes of showing off, my drunkle finally put down the baseball bat. Then later that night, things got creepy.

Instead of heading off to the bars like he always did, my drunkle stayed home and watched stupid TV show after stupid TV show on Spanish language television. By 8:45, *mi ama* had put Hernando to bed and gone to bed herself. By 9:15, Oscar had fallen asleep as well. Rodrigo had long since headed out for the evening to goodness knows where, and the only other people awake in *mi casa* were me, my drunkle, and little Miguel.

At 10:10, I saw Miguel yawn. My drunkle glanced at me with glistening eyes, and suddenly I knew exactly what he was thinking. Since I had never told anybody about our little encounter in the kitchen, my drunkle was under the impression he had a green light. It was as if my silence meant I wanted him too.

His eyes followed me as I crossed the room to put away some towels I'd just folded. I needed a plan, and quick.

"Miguel!" I suddenly snapped when I reentered the room. My shout startled him. "Did you finish your homework?"

"Huh?" he replied in a groggy state. "Yes," he added.

"Then let me see it."

"What?"

"I said, let me see it," I demanded. "Your grades have been slacking."

Miguel rubbed his eyes and marched over to his backpack. A moment later, he showed me his English essay.

"This is terrible," I said. "You can do way better. How come you don't try when it comes to school?"

"Shut up, Sonia, you're not my mother," he answered.

"No, I'm your sister," I answered. My drunkle lay on the couch listening to every word. "And I will beat your butt if you don't redo this paper right now. And do it with some effort. School is important, Miguel. It's the way out."

"The way out of what?" he asked.

"Just do your work, Miguel. I'll help you. To

answer this question properly you're going to need to write at least three paragraphs."

"Three paragraphs!?" he exclaimed. "But that will take at least forty-five minutes."

"Then you should have started sooner," I answered. My brother looked at me in complete disbelief. "It's called doing things the right way, Miguel. But don't worry, I'll sit with you till you get it done . . . even if it takes all night."

"All night?"

"Begin," I ordered.

Miguel looked up at me with uncertainty.

"Now!" I said.

Ten minutes later my drunkle got off the couch, grabbed his coat, and headed for the bars. I had escaped.

Yet, for how long?

Biting my fingernails, I went to the kitchen, opened the cabinet, and unscrewed the childproof safety top of my mother's medicine bottle.

Then I stole another little orange pill.

chapter treinta y uno

It's not uncommon with babies to find little "surprises" in their diapers. On Sunday morning, however, I found a little surprise in the babies' diaper drawer.

"What the hell is this?" I said, storming into Rodrigo's room. Even though it was almost noon, he was still asleep.

"Huh . . . what?" he replied, with messed-up hair and pillow marks on his face.

"This," I said, tossing a big bag filled with thirty-five smaller plastic baggies onto his bed. Each was filled with marijuana.

"Now you're selling it?"

"Sssh," Rodrigo said. "Tío will hear."

"What?" I replied, not giving a poop how loud my voice was. "He smokes it with you, what do you care?"

"I know," Rodrigo answered, rubbing the sleep from his eyes. "We were selling it together. But the fucking bastard is smoking all the profits," Rodrigo explained. "I had to hide it before he smoked it all."

"Are you out of your mind?" I said.

"Ssshh, he's gonna hear."

"Listen to me. You are not keeping this *mota* in the babies' diaper drawer, *me entiendes*? I'll flush it," I said. "I'll flush it all."

"But where else can I put it?" Rodrigo asked. "How about your underwear drawer? Please, Sonia. He'd never look there."

My eyes grew big as baseballs.

"I swear, I'll flush every last leaf, Rigo, you hear me? You keep that shit away, understand? Away!"

"You say that now, but if something happens to Papi, and we need the money, you'll be talking different then," my brother said as he sat up in bed.

"Nothing is happening to Papi," I answered.

"I'm just saying . . ."

"Well, don't just say! Nothing is happening to Papi," I repeated. "But I guarantee, something is gonna happen to you if I tell him what you're doing."

"You better not, Sonia."

"You know I will."

"You better not," he said again.

"Just keep that stuff away, and don't let me see it again, Rigo."

I stormed out of the room. Rodrigo didn't say anything else. Actually, he did say one more thing.

"Bitch," I heard as I left the room.

I went to the kitchen to start preparing the babies' next meal and saw that the refrigerator door was open. *Mi ama* was up and around the house these days, feeling a bit stronger. She was looking in the fridge, hoping to find some chorizo.

"Sonia, do you have to fight with your brother?" she said in a pleading voice. "Please," she added. "I'm not feeling well."

For a moment I just stood there shocked that she was reprimanding me for fighting with Rodrigo. Then I thought, Naw, it's not worth it. So I kept quiet. I didn't say anything in response to her. I just started preparing two bottles of baby formula. The twins would be up from their nap soon.

"Not too much powder," *mi ama* said as I mixed the formula. "They like it kind of watery."

How would you know, I thought. How the hell would you know?

A few hours later, *mi papi* was sitting on the couch watching a Sunday *fútbol* game, but without Rodrigo or my drunkle or any of the other boys joining him.

Everyone was off somewhere doing their own thing. The only other person in the room was *mi ama*. She was sorting through the week's mail, getting ready to pay the bills that were now up to their third late notice.

"Sonia . . ." she called while I was in the kitchen preparing dinner. *"Ayúdame."*

What now, I thought. I stepped into the living room.

"¿Qué pasa?" I asked.

"Read this for me," she said in Spanish. "It's from your school."

My school? I wiped my hands on a dish towel and took the letter. A moment later, I tossed it on the table and got ready to go back into *la cocina*.

"What does it say?" *mi ama* asked.

I turned and answered. No emotion. No guilt. No feeling whatsoever. I simply relayed to her the information I had just read.

"It says my attendance is too poor and my credits are too shy and I will not be graduating with the rest of the seniors," I told her. "It's a form letter. They don't really care about me. They just send it as a way to cover their butts so a student doesn't sue for a diploma. Did you want it for some reason?" I asked, picking the letter back up and offering it to her.

Mi ama looked at me and hesitated. She tried to say something to make me feel better.

"You should be proud of what you accomplished, *mija*. I mean, look at me, I only went to school through sixth grade. You made it much further. That is good."

I didn't answer.

"Oh, don't take it to heart, Sonia. Education isn't everything in this world. At least, not like *familia*," she continued. "It's important to remember what you've been blessed with."

I glanced over at *mi papi*, who had stopped watching his *fútbol* game and was instead staring at me. We had one of those silent conversations with only eye contact that Latinos are famous for. His eyes were sad, and he looked at me as if to say he was sorry, that he could not work any harder than he already was, and there was nothing more that he could do. My eyes looked back at him in a way that let him know I understood, that it was not his fault, that these were the cards I had been dealt in life, and I was playing them the best I could.

But still, yes, my dreams had been crushed.

After we finished our silent eye-contact conversation, I looked down at the floor. No, not even *mi papi* could save me.

"Dinner will be ready in twenty-five minutes," I said, and returned to the kitchen.

When I entered *la cocina* I noticed that the garbage was full, so I pulled the plastic bag out of its container and took the trash outside. The evening was warm and a bit muggy. When I threw open the top of the Dumpster, flies buzzed around my head. I waved them away, tossed the garbage inside, and closed the top. Then I thought about Geraldo.

"What a disgusting place to have a romance anyway," I said to myself, trying to avoid the horrible smell. "Funny, I never remember all these bugs."

I was sure with all the time that had passed, Geraldo had long since moved on. He'd probably found a new girl. Maybe ten of them. I always knew that he could do so much better than me.

"It's good for him," I told myself. "Better for him this way. After all, if you love somebody, set them free, right? I would have only been a ball and chain to Geraldo, getting in the way of all his big dreams."

Just then Frijolito walked up and started rubbing against my leg. I bent down and scratched him in his favorite place, right behind his ear with the weak muscle. Though he was a lot older and no longer a kitten, Frijolito still had a big ol' lump in his belly and walked kind of sideways.

He purred.

"I bet you're ready for dinner, huh?" I said.

I hesitated. Deep in my heart I was hoping that, just like in a magical love story, I would suddenly hear a velvety voice behind me that would say something dashing, something romantic like, "And I bet you are ready for dinner too, like a Snickers bar and a cup of vegetable soup . . . in Paris, France!"

I so badly needed to hear a few words that would lighten my heart and sweep me off my feet. So, so badly.

I raised my eyes and squinted into the light of the orange sunset, hoping with all the hope I had left in my soul that the boy with the emerald green eyes and a glistening white smile would be staring warmly at me, magically promising to take me away, just like in fairy tales.

I looked up. All I saw were flies. No, *Príncipe* Charming did not exist. Fairy tales were bullshit.

I stood, went to the garage, filled up the bowl I kept hidden for Frijolito behind the old bicycles no one rode anymore, and went back inside *mi casa*.

Besides, I couldn't leave for Paris anyway. I mean, how could I? I had beans on the stove.

chapter treinta y dos

On Tuesday morning we got a call that my drunkle had been arrested again. For the same crime, too— attempting to steal a car stereo out of a BMW. This time, though, there would be no pink citations. He was going to have to appear in front of a judge.

Mi ama dragged me to court on Thursday morning so that I could interpret what was going on for her and Tía Luna. And the twins would be coming too. I thought about leaving them with Rodrigo for the day, but I instantly knew that would be a bad idea. I'd probably come home to find them wearing their onesies outfits with their heads through the armholes while sitting in dirty, stinky diapers. I could just see it: my brother lying on the couch, stoned out of his mind, watching cartoons, and pretending he hadn't realized the twins needed their diapers changed, even though the smell of baby poop would have been bad enough to melt the paint off the walls.

No, I was taking the twins.

It was a day of firsts for the babies. It was their first time on a bus, their first time trekking across the city, their first time being hassled by the police. It happened at the courthouse. Going through security at the entrance of the building was a total nightmare. They made us wake two napping babies and remove them from their strollers while people with badges and guns checked our blankets, diaper bags, and even our formula. What did they think, that people hid bombs inside bottles of baby milk? Maybe white babies were being checked too, but I have a feeling that if they were, the guards certainly weren't being incredibly rude to the parents as they did so. It took us fifteen minutes just to get inside the building, and then once we were in, we were informed that we were in the wrong courthouse.

"This is civil court. What you need is the criminal courthouse across the street," a uniformed woman told us.

Great, I thought. You couldn't have mentioned that before you strip-searched the sleeping infants?

With a huge sigh we turned around, exited the building, and waited for the traffic light to change so we could cross the street. Of course I was the one pushing the made-for-two stroller. Though it had been months since giving birth, *mi ama* still didn't have her physical strength all the way back, and my aunt, well, Tía Luna was so fat she practically needed a stroller for her own big, bubble-butt self. (And Lord help the person who had to push that thing!)

While we waited at the light, a brand-new white Lexus pulled up, being driven by two white men. Probably lawyers, I thought, by the way they were dressed.

The one in the passenger seat looked at me then said something to his friend. A moment later the driver turned and looked at me, too. Then they both laughed. Though the windows were up, I could tell that I had just become the butt of some sort of "look-at-how-young-these-Mexican-girls-pump-out-babies" joke.

A moment later the light turned green and they drove away.

Oh, how I hated being a stereotype. I felt like chasing after them to explain, *Hey, these aren't my kids.*

Then again, yeah, they kinda were. I lowered my eyes and crossed the street. Even when you aren't a stereotype, to some people you still are.

After going through security a second time where they checked the babies for nuclear warheads and rocket grenade launchers, we entered the correct building and set off to find my drunkle. After three-and-a-half hours of sitting on hard, wooden benches, my drunkle's case was finally brought before the judge.

They led him into the courtroom in handcuffs. My drunkle was wearing a bright orange jumpsuit that said PRISONER in big, black letters, and slip-on shoes that had no laces in them so he couldn't commit suicide by hanging himself while in custody. (Not that I would have minded if he did.) My drunkle looked unshaven, messy, and smelly . . . pretty much like he always did. The bailiff walked him to a chair, motioned him to sit, and the proceeding began.

Things started with the judge. Then the lawyer spoke.

"What's he saying?" *mi ama* asked.

"He asked, How does he plead? And *Tío's* lawyer just said 'not guilty.'"

"Not guilty, that's good," Tía Luna said in Spanish as she leaned in and listened to my words. Then the prosecutor spoke. I translated.

"He says, 'Bail should be denied. Enough is enough,'" I interpreted. "He says there's no way we should let this man back out on our streets. He's a repeat offender, he's got multiple outstanding warrants, and he's doesn't even have the required papers to be in this country. The chances of flight are very high."

"*Racistas,*" my aunt said. "They're all racists."

The public defender responded.

"Correct me if I am wrong, but the last time I checked, in the United States of America, this man is entitled to the presumption of innocence and due process. Your Honor, my client deserves his rights."

"And what about the rights of tax-paying American citizens?" answered the prosecutor in a fiery tone. "Who is representing them? This man is an illegal. This man is a criminal. This man is a burden on society in many, many ways. Hospitals, jails, the insurance prices we pay—what doesn't this type of person negatively affect for the average American?"

"Might I remind my esteemed colleague of a small little document called the Constitution?" answered the public defender. "To not treat my client in the same manner that all people who appear before this court are treated, regardless of race, color, or creed, is an affront to everything our founding fathers stood for."

"Enough, gentleman, enough," interrupted the

judge as he rubbed his temples. "You're giving me a headache."

I looked over at my drunkle. I knew he didn't understand a word of what was going on, but still, he sat there looking as if he really couldn't give a damn. The lack of respect he showed for the courts, for the lawyers, for the entire judicial process was plain for all to see. My drunkle had been to jail before in both El Norte and Mexico, and he didn't look as if he was sweating the outcome of this arraignment either way.

¿Lo que será será, right?

It turned out that this time the "stupid" American courts denied my drunkle bail.

"*Racistas,*" Tía Luna said when she heard the judge's verdict.

"But, Your Honor, if I may . . ." said the public defender.

"I've made my decision, counselor. Next case. I've got about a thousand more to get through before we end for the day."

The lawyers closed their briefcases and the bailiff led my drunkle, still in handcuffs, behind the wooden door through which they had entered. A moment later he disappeared.

"*¿Qué pasa?*" *mi ama* asked. "What happens now?"

"*Yo no sé,*" I answered, telling her I didn't know. The public defender grabbed his briefcase and started walking out of the courtroom. I chased after him.

"Excuse me, what's going to happen to that man you just defended?" I asked in English. The public defender kept walking, not even breaking stride.

"I'll plea him out for a lesser charge. With his record, he's probably looking at twenty-eight to thirty-six months in jail. Why, who are you?"

"Family," I answered.

"Sorry," he said.

I stopped walking alongside of him.

"Yeah, me too."

The lawyer entered an elevator, started dialing his cell phone, and vanished behind closed doors.

On the way home, *mi ama* had to search for enough coins for the bus while I wrestled with getting the twins loaded and down the aisle. However, as *mi ama* and Tía Luna could clearly see, I wasn't nearly as annoyed with all the little aggravations on the way home from court as I had been on the way *to* court.

We found some seats toward the back of the bus. My aunt stared at me as we bounced along in the plastic seats.

"*¿Qué?*" I finally asked.

"*Es familia*," she said to me. "What kind of person is happy when a member of *la familia* is sent to prison?"

I lowered my eyes and didn't answer. But she was right: I was definitely happy.

chapter treinta y tres

For the first three days after my drunkle was sent to jail, I was still tense while walking around *mi casa*, but soon the pressure started to lighten. I don't think I quite realized how much the presence of my drunkle had been weighing on me. But once he was gone, it was like I could breathe again.

I realized that I hadn't sent an e-mail to Maria in quite a while. I had to admit that it was totally lame that I hadn't at least sent her a small hello, so instead of shooting her off a note of apology, I went to the bookstore and bought Isabella a book on baby sign language. After all, sign language is a legitimate, real language, like Portuguese or French, and if Isabella learned how to sign, I figured she'd able to communicate with a whole bunch of people later in life. Any small advantage had to help, right?

Inside the package I added a twenty dollar bill and a small note telling Maria that I hoped she was not offended by my sending her this book, and that the *pocha* aunt from California was just trying to help out any way she could. I walked out of the post office after mailing Isabella her gift and my heart felt lighter. It was nice to do nice things for other people. It really was true what my favorite bumper sticker of all time said: MEAN PEOPLE SUCK.

When I got back from the post office, I called Tee-Ay.

It turned out that Constancy had long since given birth, and Tee had been accepted to the University of Southern California after a whole lot of drama. Her story was absolutely incredible. We were on the phone for over two hours, and after I hung up, I felt even better about the world. As Tee-Ay told me, life worked just like that stupid little sign on Mr. Wardin's wall in history class said it did: GOOD THINGS HAPPEN TO PEOPLE WHO TRY.

While my spirits were much higher after I hung up with Tee, they still weren't high enough for me to call Geraldo. And truthfully, I didn't think I ever would. What was gone was gone, and I had to be a realist about that. But hearing Tee-Ay's story did inspire me to do something I didn't think I ever would.

* * *

"Do you remember me?" I asked. Bright and early on Monday morning I had gone to school.

"No," said Mrs. Javellano. "I mean, I remember your face, but I see a lot of students. What was your name again?"

"Sonia," I answered. "Sonia Rodriguez."

"Oh, I remember. Home studies, right?"

"I did the first packet," I said, pulling out the work sheets she had given me a long time ago. "I know, it's a little late."

"Yeah," she said sarcastically. "Just a little."

"But is it too late?" I asked with hope in my voice.

Mrs. Javellano swiveled in her chair, took the packets from me, and looked at my work. I may have been preposterously tardy with the assignment, but every problem was done in its entirety and I was sure that each answer was absolutely correct. I had even double-checked all my spelling and made sure to answer all the questions in complete sentences that were properly punctuated.

"It's never *too* late, *mija*," Mrs. Javellano said as she set down my work. "Maybe we can work something out so that you'll be able to graduate next year."

"I would like to graduate," I answered. "With my class."

"With the seniors this year?" she replied with a laugh. "I don't think that's possible."

"You don't think that's possible, or you think that you don't think that's possible but it might be possible?" I asked with a very serious look in my eye.

Mrs. Javellano paused and studied the determination on my face. But still, I could see she was doubtful.

"I'm willing to work hard," I added.

"How hard?" she asked. That small opening was all I needed.

"Very hard," I answered. "Very, very, very hard."

Still, Mrs. Javellano stared.

"I mean, we've got to get more Latinas walking these halls with diplomas instead of babies, right?" I then added, throwing back in her face the same line she had used on me.

Mrs. Javellano stared for another moment, then, without a word, stood up, smoothed out her fashionable red pants, and crossed the room to her file cabinet.

"I'm not making any promises, *mija*. Do this and we'll talk," she said as she handed me a huge stack of papers.

I think Mrs. Javellano expected me to be intimidated by the large amount of work she had just handed me. I flipped through the folder. There was science, math, English, and history assignments all rolled together in one big package.

"By tomorrow," she said in a strict tone. She informed me that the amount of work she had just given to me was supposed to take the average home-studies student two weeks to finish.

I didn't flinch. The next day, I was back in her office ready for more.

Mrs. Javellano looked over the work I had done. I watched her as she took notice of the fact that each and every problem had been done correctly and neatly. Some people don't think neatness counts, but it does.

"It's good, but this is not a one-night stand," Mrs. Javellano commented as if she were trying for a second time to scare me off. She handed me another giant bundle of assignments. I thanked her and then returned the following day with every last bit of work done. I returned a third day, too, but this time with two things for Mrs. Javellano: the first was the homework packet with every problem correctly solved. Home studies might not have been the most academically challenging work there was, but there certainly was a lot of it. I guess it had to be that way so I could make up all those missing credits in a short amount of time.

Number two, I brought Mrs. Javellano a home-made *champurrado vainilla*. After all, who doesn't like to start their day off with a little hot vanilla drink to take the chill out of the air?

Mrs. Javellano didn't accept my *champurrado*, though. Instead, she told me it was unnecessary and somewhat inappropriate for a student to bring her a morning drink as if she could be bribed. Then in a firm tone she said, "Now, do this," and handed me an even bigger pile for day four.

"I know," I answered with a forced smile. "By tomorrow."

That day, she didn't even smile back. She was all business.

For the next two weeks I showed up every morning bright and early at 7:10 with a large stack of work and two *champurrados vainillas*. And even though I was up every night until at least 2:00, I never felt tired. After three weeks, I'd only missed one question, and I'd gotten perfect scores on all my tests.

"Well, you certainly are persistent, Sonia, I'll give you that," she said as she took a sip of the drink I had brought her. By week three, Mrs. Javellano had started bringing muffins so that the two of us could share a small breakfast while she graded my work. I liked the blueberry ones best.

"Here you go," she said as she handed me my next stack of work.

"Mrs. Javellano?" I said.

"¿Sí, Sonia?"

"Would it be possible for you to give me everything so that I could just get it done once and for all?" I asked before she closed her file cabinet. "It's a holiday weekend, and I could make some good progress."

Mrs. Javellano laughed.

"It's Cinco de Mayo, *mija*. Why don't you take a break and spend some time with your *familia*?" she offered. "You've worked hard."

"I don't want to take a break," I said. "I want to be *la primera*."

There was a pause. Mrs. Javellano studied me and then put down her drink.

"I was *la primera*," she said.

"You were the first, too?" I answered back.

"*Sí*, not just high school, but also college," she told me. "I started at community college then transferred to a four-year university and then went on to get a master's degree."

"A master's degree?" I said. "I don't think I can—"

"Yes, you can, *mija*," Mrs. Javellano interrupted forcefully. "*Sí, tú puedes.* And you must never think you can't."

A moment later Mrs. Javellano crossed the room, went to her file cabinet, and pulled out eight thick packets. My arms sank when she handed them to me.

But inside I smiled. I was only eight packets away from being the first Rodriguez in America to graduate from high school.

Me, the *tortuguita*.

chapter treinta y cuatro

No one in *mi familia* was nearly as religious as Tía Luna, and she always tried to make us feel guilty about it around holidays like Easter and El Día de la Candelaria, the day that Mary first presented Jesus in church. Year after year my aunt wanted to celebrate religious holidays much more devotedly than the rest of us. Heck, if it had been up to her, we'd have put a fifty-foot Christ-on-the-crucifix on the top of our roof for Good Friday and spent the next seventy-two hours until el Domingo de Resurrección flogging ourselves on the front lawn.

But when it came to Cinco de Mayo, the only real Mexican holiday in El Norte, our entire *familia* was always excited to go full speed ahead. It was our absolute favorite day of the year. The food, *las horchatas*, the dancing, *las piñatas*, the fireworks, *la música*—our whole street would close down so that every family on the block could participate in *una Gran Fiesta* of cultural pride. Hundreds of people would show up to celebrate. It was a real sight to see. Women would be dressed in bright, flowing dresses, while men like *mi papi* would wear traditional *charro* suits, dressing like fine Western cowboys with giant sombreros and shiny, thick boots. We had *mariachi* bands, dancers who would swirl and stomp their feet, delicious foods that seemed to never run out, and lots and lots of smiles and love in the air. As *mi ama* once told me, more than one baby was made on the night of Cinco de Mayo in our neighborhood, that was for sure. It was as if *amor* floated inside the oxygen we breathed. Cinco de Mayo was the only day of the year that offered something for everyone in our household.

And this year it was going to offer me the opportunity to earn my diploma. Doing all those packets made me feel like some kind of marathon runner who was getting stronger and stronger as I got closer and closer to the finish line. In my mind, Cinco de Mayo came every year, but the chance to graduate high school on time with the rest of my class only came once. I was determined to do it and made plans to stay home.

Plus, this year was a little weird anyway. Tía Luna was still depressed about the fact that my drunkle was in jail, and *mi papi* had chosen to work instead of taking the whole night off to come to the fiesta. Last year his gym had to close down because there were no Mexicans to clean the locker rooms—everyone had called in sick to go out and party (including *mi papi*)—so this year the gym offered Papi double-time wages, a seventy-five dollar bonus, and an extra night off later that week if he would work. After all, the gym had to stay open for the white people who didn't know the difference between Cinco de Mayo and Día de los Muertos.

It was just too much of a good deal for *mi papi* to pass up, despite the fact that for the past sixteen years he had dressed up in a full Mexican *charro* costume and ridden horses with three of his *compadres* in the city's annual midnight Cinco de Mayo parade. But this year, *mi papi* would not be able to join his friends. They said they understood; after all, a real *vato* had to do what he had to do to support his *familia*, but Papi still packed up a bag of clothes just in case he had the chance to get off work early, change outfits at the gym, and ride a horse in the holiday parade after his shift ended. One way or another, Papi would still get in some good fun, because Cinco de Mayo parties always went on very late into the evening; but still, he was hoping not to break his *tradición*.

Tradiciones are big in the Hispanic community.

Lucky for me, Ama was feeling better, so she decided to take the twins out to the street fair in the made-for-two stroller. Besides, when you're a Latina, nothing gets you more positive attention than going out with a cute little baby, and *mi ama* had two of them. With the way I'd dressed them, in adorable, matching, mini-mariachi outfits, *mi ama* would be the toast of the town all night long. It was the perfect opportunity for me to stay home and get some real work done in peace and quiet.

I held the front door open for *mi ama* as she rolled the babies outside.

"Sonia, come, have some *nieve de fresa*," she said to me in Spanish. "It's your favorite." There was a spark of real happiness in her eyes. "And Cinco de Mayo is your favorite holiday."

"*No, gracias, Ama.* Maybe I'll go later with Papi when he comes home after work," I answered. Though I admit I was tempted by the thought of *nieve de fresa*, I was more excited to stay home alone and get my work done.

My two younger brothers Oscar and Miguel dashed out the door. They would be out until well after midnight, eating sugary foods and causing trouble like all the other boys their age, and they were as jumpy as jelly beans with excitement. Rodrigo, of course, had long since left for the evening. *Mi ama* took the twins, Tía Luna took my two-year-old brother, Hernando, and everyone exited. I closed the front door and made myself a cup of hot tea.

Mmm, spiced cinnamon.

After changing into some clothes that were a bit more comfortable, I sat down, turned on my study light, and smiled. A proud feeling came over me as I thought about my younger brothers and sister. I realized I was like one of those trekkers in the forest, hacking my way through thick brush with a machete; and while it had certainly been tough for me, *mis hermanos y hermana* would have a clearly marked road to follow and a much easier time getting through, now that I was almost done. Sure, the twins were babies, but babies grow up, and I wanted them to have a good life with the good opportunities education offered.

And don't think I wasn't going to bust Oscar's and Miguel's butts either. Sure, they were out playing tonight, but next week, I was determined to pound them like a crazy person about school. In El Norte, *escuela* matters.

Forty-five minutes later I finished the packet of math. Thirty minutes after that I completed the science section. Then I got a bug up my butt to take a break and I went to the old computer *mi papi* had been given by his white boss when they did their technology upgrade last year, unplugged the home phone line, and jammed it into to the side of the tan machine so that I could go online and check my e-mail. I was hoping that Maria had gotten the sign language book I had sent.

Though my Internet connection was as slow as ketchup being poured out of a bottle, I finally got online, and sure enough, there was an e-mail from Maria.

Hola pocha,

Got the book . . . awesome gift! (And of course, no offense taken.)

Isabella seems to be a natural at sign language. She's already learned how to say milk, bath and banana. Seems Abuelita knows some sign lang. too.

This week she taught Isabella how to give someone the middle finger. Abuelita says it's because folks can be cruel in this world, and a deaf baby is going to need to know how to tell a person to fuck off.

I must say, I kind of agree with her.

Am I a bad mother for allowing my daughter
to learn that?

How's school, Rigo, the rest of the family,
and, most important, your mysterious love
life, which you never tell me about? Anytime
you get the urge to do the in-and-out,
remember, there's a caballero down here who
would drive across three borders to be your
partner. :-)

Miss you, hug you, love you!!

Maria

p.s. Come visit soon—we'll bathe like mermaids
again. LOL!!

I couldn't help but smile. Though it had been a
while, *mi prima* and I were still connected like two peas
in a pod and I wondered when the next time I could visit
would be. I figured I'd run the idea by *mi ama* in the
morning and type a reply to Maria after I had an
answer. Truly, I couldn't wait to head back to Abuelita's
and take wee-wees with bullfrogs the size of buffalo.

There's just something about the place that gets
under your skin. In a good way, though.

I returned to the table, sat back down under my
study light, and opened the next packet. Break time
was over. Suddenly I heard a noise.

"*Hola,*" I called out.

It sounded like a key turning the lock. There was no reply.

"*¿Quién es?*" I said, asking "Who's there?'

The door slammed open, and a moment later my dirty, greasy drunkle stumbled through the front door.

No, he hadn't escaped from prison. He's too stupid to pull off anything like that. The jails simply set him free due to overcrowding. It's called the catch-and-release program. In California, with so many inmates and not enough cells to keep everyone who's been convicted of a crime locked up, "minor" offenses (and in Los Angeles, "minor" means anything less than first-degree serial murder with a chain saw) are let out of jail to free up prison beds. Due to recent budget cuts and overpopulation, the cell doors of almost thirteen hundred inmates had been let open to make room for the next wave of prisoners. So-called "minor" offenders like my drunkle got released with time served. Even illegals set for deportation hearings were set free. My drunkle had served twenty-two days of a thirty-one-month sentence and been given a sheet of paper with a citation to appear in front of an immigration committee to determine whether or not he would be allowed to stay in this country.

And yes, it was pink.

His hearing had been set for four months from now. My drunkle crumpled the sheet of paper and laughed.

"*Adivina quién regressssssó?*" he asked with a bit of flair for the dramatic. In English it translated as, "Guess who's baaaaack?"

He was drunk. I was wearing only a nightgown. He looked around, saw that I was alone, and began to walk toward me. I froze with terror.

chapter treinta y cinco

"You've been teasing me," he said in Spanish. "For too long. But I know you feel our attraction."

I could tell by the look in his eyes that he was hungry, very hungry, but for something other than food. Fireworks from the celebration exploded outside. He moved closer.

"*Es una fiesta,*" he said with glowing, bloodshot eyes. "And tonight will be ours."

He violently grabbed me, pulled me close. My drunkle was a strong man, and I knew instantly that I was no match for him physically. And emotionally, I had no will to fight. Deep in my heart it was my worst fear coming to life. I could do *nada*, nothing, other than watch it happen, as if it were a movie and I was viewing the horrifying drama of someone else.

A part of me always knew that this day would

come. And a part of me also knew that my voice would fail me when it did. I didn't scream for help. Instead, like a coward, I submitted.

He began to take off my nightgown. I wished for the ability to do something, but I couldn't. Terror had frozen me, stolen my ability to act. I was his puppet and my drunkle knew it.

He reached for my top button. Then the second. Then the third. Though I was wearing a bra, it was low cut and my breasts were partially exposed. He smiled. I could tell that he liked what he saw very much.

My drunkle paused and took a moment to enjoy the sick pleasure of it all. A few hours earlier he'd been locked in a cage like a beast and now he was in *mi casa*, about to enjoy the pleasures of my young flesh. The tip of his tongue slithered from his mouth like a snake, and he licked his lips as if preparing for a delicious meal. Ready to continue on, his oily, black fingernails reached for the bottom of my nightgown. His filthy hand lightly brushed against the skin of my naked thigh. I took a deep breath and closed my eyes.

I thought again about fighting back. I wanted to fight back. I wished for the ability to fight back, but still I was too afraid. It was as if the practically-an-adult Sonia had completely vanished and all that was left was the itty-bitty-girl Sonia, the one who was horribly freaked out and too scared to move. Yes, I wanted to act heroically, but I didn't. I couldn't. Fear had swallowed me like that whale Moby Dick in the famous book. I just didn't have the courage to defend myself.

His finger started to work its way up my leg. My heart beat a thousand miles a minute. I felt the heat of his body as he stepped closer.

Suddenly the front door flew open with a crash. My drunkle and I turned our heads at the same time.

It was Geraldo.

"There will be no more," he said. *"No más."*

It turns out that after I first broke up with Geraldo, he'd spent night after night watching me through the cheap drapes of my front window. Though he never made himself known, he often looked at me by the light of my study lamp with great longing. But after a while, he gave up his long bus rides across the city to stare at me like a stalker in the night. However, today was May fifth, and once upon a time I had made a promise to him about my lips being his birthday present.

He'd come to collect. Months may have passed, but his love for me still burned like a roaring flame.

My drunkle, when he realized who the boy was, pushed me away like a rag doll.

"You fucking Central," my drunkle said in disbelief that Geraldo had had the nerve to enter his house. Geraldo didn't respond with words. Instead he balled up his fists. The two of them lunged at each other.

The battle was no match at all. My drunkle had learned how to fight dirty in prison and in a matter of moments he had punched Geraldo in the balls, thumbed him in the eye, and put him in a staggering, choking headlock. A pair of scissors lay on the table. A second later they were in my drunkle's hand, then at Geraldo's throat, my drunkle preparing to slash Geraldo's neckline ear to ear.

"Now I'm going to slice you like the *cerote* pig you are," he said with a growl. It sounded like a threat from the devil himself.

My drunkle raised the blade.

"No!" I shouted. Somehow, my voice had returned. "Please. I'll do anything. Whatever you want."

My drunkle looked up. To prove I was serious, I lowered the nightgown off my shoulder.

"And I will do it over and over," I said. "Have me now. Have me tomorrow. Have me whenever you want. You can have me for years, I swear, I'll never tell anyone. Just please, don't."

I looked up at Geraldo, whose face was turning red from a lack of oxygen.

"Don't," I repeated. "Please."

My drunkle paused. Geraldo's eyes glared at me with wild desperation. The look on his face was clear: *No, don't do it, Sonia. NO!*

I ignored Geraldo. A wicked smile slowly crept over my drunkle's face.

"Hear that, *cerote* pig? You need a girl to save you."

Sfffftt! My drunkle slashed a half-inch slice behind Geraldo's ear. Blood squirted on the floor.

"As a reminder," my drunkle said, and then he grabbed a candlestick and punched Geraldo in the head with it.

It didn't kill him, but my drunkle had knocked him unconscious. Geraldo fell to the floor like a bag of bricks.

Suddenly the house fell eerily quiet. Fiesta music and dancing could be heard outside. Laughter echoed from the streets. My drunkle stood, crossed the room, and turned off the study light so that no one else would be able to see inside.

Click. The lamp went out.

"I always knew you wanted me," my drunkle said in Spanish as he closed the front door. *"Ven aquí,"* he ordered. "Come here."

I lowered my eyes and did what he asked. My feet

shuffled closer. When I got next to him, though, he didn't touch me; my drunkle just stared, waiting for me to do what I had promised. Slowly, I reached back to unhook my bra, but in my heart I knew I was lying.

Yes, my drunkle could have me right then, but that would be it. In my mind I'd always feared this day would come, which was why I had stolen so many of *mi ama*'s pills. I had a stash of seventeen of them wrapped inside a piece of tissue paper, hidden underneath the kitchen sink. With a warm bath and a little tequila to wash them down, it would all end.

I became numb, eyes without any light, a body without a soul. In a state of total emptiness, I surrendered.

"*¿Qué pasa?*" came a voice.

I turned. It was Papi. He was dressed like a Mexican nobleman in traditional *charro* clothing. The green jewels on his cowboy jacket sparkled, his boots shined, and he wore a gigantic sombrero, which sat proudly on his head. With his furry mustache and a squint in his eye, *mi papi* looked handsome, elegant, and fierce. It was like I was staring at a beautiful illusion.

"*Dije, ¿qué pasa?*" he asked again, and then he turned on the light. The gym still hadn't had enough Mexicans to operate so they had decided to turn the evening into Navidad number two and wax the racquetball courts. *Mi papi* had come to take me, whether I wanted to or not, for a study break, for *nieve de fresa* before he joined his *compadres* on horseback in the parade.

I was too numb to say anything. Dream world and reality had crossed over too many times.

"I caught this *cerote* pig in your house," my drunkle quickly responded. "He was about to take advantage of your daughter."

Mi papi paused and studied the situation.

"This boy?" he asked after a long moment of just staring.

"*Sí,*" said my drunkle. "This Central."

Papi looked at me. I was paralyzed, unable to speak.

"Lift his head," *mi papi* ordered.

My drunkle paused, not comprehending. Papi turned and went to his closet.

"I said, lift his head," *mi papi* repeated. A moment later my father stepped out of the closet, holding his Roberto Clemente baseball bat.

My drunkle smiled. Once again he had out-smarted his *estúpido* brother-in-law.

My drunkle crossed the room, got down on his knees, and lifted the unconscious head of Geraldo so that *mi papi* could smash him with the baseball bat.

"*Buena,*" said *mi papi* as he lined up his swing. "Hold him right there."

I started to panic, but still I was too stricken with fear to get any words out of my mouth. *Mi papi* reached back.

Use your voice, Sonia, I said to myself. *Use your voice.*

I needed to say something.

Now! I screamed inside my head. *Use your voice!* My father began to swing with full force.

USE YOUR . . .

But I was too late. My voice didn't come.

SMASH! Mi papi blasted his target. The Roberto Clemente bat broke in two. My drunkle fell to the ground like a sack of beans.

"*¡Mentiroso!*" shouted *mi papi*. "Liar!!"

SMASH! Mi papi bashed my drunkle a second time with the broken half of the bat he still held in his hand. *Mi papi* then started beating him with anything he could grab.

"*¡Bastardo!*" screamed *mi papi* as he kicked my drunkle in the ribs. Desperate to get away, my drunkle crawled out the front door of our house and stumbled into the street.

"I'll kill you!" Papi shouted as he ripped a guitar from the hands of a passing mariachi player and smashed it over my drunkle's back. Suddenly the streets fell silent, and a circle formed around *mi papi* as he began beating my drunkle in the center of the street. With the *música* stopped, the crowd grew bigger to watch.

"You think I'm a fool?" shouted *mi papi* in Spanish. "You dare to touch my daughter?"

My father kicked my drunkle again, this time in the face. There was a loud thump. Blood squirted onto *mi papi*'s boots, and my drunkle groaned in pain.

Word quickly spread throughout the crowd as to why this beating was taking place. Normally folks would have interfered, they would have stepped in to break up the fight, but when *la gente* gained a sense of why *mi papi*, a man with a reputation of great restraint, was involved in this action, no one dared move forward to halt him. The crowd just watched. It was *justicia*. Justice. Nothing was more sacred than *familia*.

My father stripped off his belt.

"You dare to touch my little girl?"

My drunkle lay there beaten, bleeding, and defenseless. He had taken too many blows to the head and though he tried to put his hands up, there was no fight left in him. *Mi papi* stepped behind him, cinched his belt around my drunkle's neck, and began to squeeze.

And squeeze.

My drunkle started to turn red. Then blue. Oxygen was being cut off from his brain and though his hands tried to grab on to the leather strap around his neck, there was nothing he could do to stop from being choked.

Mi papi yanked the belt tighter and tighter and even though there were at least 150 witnesses, no one would have said anything to the *policía* about how my drunkle had died. Some things were sacred in our community, and my drunkle had gone too far.

Too far.

His eyes began to bulge. His face turned from blue to purple. A few more seconds and my drunkle would die. I stepped through the crowd.

"No, Papi," I said in a soft voice.

My father looked up.

"No," I repeated. "Do not stoop to that level."

Papi paused. A moment later a soft look came to his eyes. He knew I was right. A second later he released the belt. My drunkle dropped to the ground like a hunk of meat and sucked in a breath of air.

I stepped forward and hugged my father. *Mi papi* squeezed me back.

"*Te quiero, Papi,*" I said. A tear came to his eyes.

"I love you too, *tortuguita.*"

Papi dropped the belt. It was over. It was all over.

I looked up, and *mi ama's* face appeared through the crowd. She exchanged looks with my father and lowered her eyes in shame. A moment after that Tía Luna appeared with her mouth open, ready to shout something when she saw the state of my drunkle. Then, when her eyes met my father's, she too lowered her gaze. The fierceness of his glare had frightened both of them into instant submission.

"Return, you die," Papi said to my drunkle. My drunkle stumbled to his feet and scampered off like a beaten, bloody dog, never to be seen again. Hugging me, *mi papi* walked us through the silent and stunned crowd and we went back inside our *casa.*

chapter treinta y seis

After *mi papi* and I had taken Geraldo to the emergency room and sent him home, we returned to our house.

Mi papi picked up the broken handle of what was left of his Roberto Clemente bat and looked around at the mess. Everyone in *la casa* had returned home after having heard about what had happened. Bad news like this made its way around a Latino community quicker than cold cheese melted on a hot enchilada.

Rodrigo, *mi ama*, Oscar, me, Tía Luna, Miguel, Hernando, even the twins, sat in the living room and waited, not knowing what Papi was going to do.

He picked up a glass of water and took a long, slow sip. Then *smash!* he threw the glass down in the center of the room where it exploded into a thousand pieces. Everyone jumped back in fear.

"You," he said, as he pointed the tip of the broken baseball bat at Rodrigo, "will get a job. That is, after you get down on your hands and knees and wash the blood and clean the glass off this floor."

Mi papi breathed deeply, his nostrils going in and out like an angry bull.

"I always believed actions spoke louder than *palabras*," he continued. "But I was wrong. Words are now needed in this *casa*, too."

Rodrigo looked up in shock.

"You don't like it?" *mi papi* said. "There's the door. You can follow your piece-of-shit uncle."

Papi stared with a steel glare. Rodrigo lowered his eyes.

"Well . . . I'm waiting," said *mi papi*.

With his head down, Rodrigo stood, went to the kitchen, and grabbed a damp towel. A moment later he was down on his hands and knees scrubbing up blood.

"And I mean every last drop. If there is even a speck of red . . ." *Mi papi* didn't need to complete his sentence. Rodrigo understood exactly what he meant. Papi then turned to my two younger brothers Oscar and Miguel.

"*Hijos, vengan aquí,*" he commanded. My brothers looked up with terror in their eyes. Papi led them into his bedroom. They followed along silently.

"I want both of you to clean up the mess in here," Papi ordered. My brothers looked around, confused.

"Uhm, what mess?" Oscar finally asked.

"This one," answered Papi, and with one giant swing of his Roberto Clemente baseball bat, *mi papi* smashed *mi ama*'s television set into a million pieces. Glass flew everywhere.

Though she was seated in the living room, the violent crash from the bedroom caused Ama to jump back in gigantic fright.

"Now get going," *mi papi* ordered. "And if your grades in school don't improve in the next few weeks, both of you will taste the belt, ¿*me entienden?*"

My brothers leaped into action, terrified of what might happen to them next. Once the two of them had started working, *mi papi* stepped out of the bedroom and stared fiercely at Ama. She sat with Tía Luna on the couch, shaking with fear, wondering what—or who—*mi papi* was going to break next.

"Your television seems to have a small technical problem," Papi explained. "Looks like no *telenovelas* for a while."

His message was clear: stop using Sonia as a servant. *Mi ama* said nothing; she just kept her head down. Papi went to the front door and opened it.

"This is a doorbell," he said to Tía Luna. My aunt was so scared, the fat on her neck jiggled. "And this is how you use it," *mi papi* explained.

He pushed the little button. *Bing-bong*.

"Sometimes, when people do not answer, it means they are not home," *mi papi* continued. "And even when it looks like there are people at home, sometimes they're really not. Do you understand this technology?" he asked.

Tía Luna nodded and looked at the floor.

"Then why don't you try it the next time you come over?" *mi papi* suggested as he held open the front door. He waited. It took Tía Luna a moment to realize that he was kicking her out of the house. Slowly she pushed her fat butt off the couch, picked up her purse, and exited without a word about Jesus, the devil, or the future of our burning souls.

"Thank you for visiting," *mi papi* said as he closed the door behind her. "We look forward to seeing you soon."

He then spun around.

"Sonia," he barked in a firm voice. It was his loudest command yet. I looked up, ready to be scolded like everyone else.

"*Lo siento,*" *mi papi* said gently.

I paused.

"I am sorry," he repeated. "Truly sorry."

"It's not your fault, Papi," I answered in Spanish. "It's mine."

"No!" he snapped. "It's not. Don't ever think like that. It is not your fault." He stared across the room at *mi ama*. "It is ours," he said. "It is ours."

I saw wetness forming in *mi papi*'s eyes. Of all the jobs he did, he'd always felt that job number one was to be a great father, and right then I could see that he felt that he had failed.

"I . . . I never realized," *mi papi* said, shaking his head. "With all the time I was working, I thought I was making things better." He paused. "But I was not."

He looked down at the floor. "I was not."

I wanted to say something to him, to let him know that it was okay, that things would be all right and that he really was a great *papi*. But I could tell he didn't want to be comforted at the moment. It was like he wanted to experience the pain, as if he deserved it, for some reason. A teardrop fell from his eye. I could do nothing other than let him experience the great hurt. But I felt sad for him. So sad that I wanted to cry myself.

"*Mañana*," Papi added, wiping away a tear. "*Tú vas a la escuela*," he told me. He looked over at *mi ama* and repeated his words. "Tomorrow, Sonia, you go to school and finish what you need."

My mother didn't look up.

"And I promise, *mija*, if it takes me to my last breath, I will make things right," he said. "I will make things right."

It was only the second time in my entire life I had seen *mi papi* cry, and the first time had only been a few hours earlier when he was about to strangle my drunkle in the middle of the street. But I saw him cry a third time, too. At my high-school graduation.

The event was incredible. *Mi* entire *familia* came, and each of them beamed with pride. Even Rodrigo was proud of me. *Dios mío*, he even wore a tie.

Okay, *mi papi* had forced him to, but still, Rigo was proud. I could also tell he was sad too. He sort of looked regretful the whole time, like, if he had known the pride he could have brought to himself and *la familia* by earning his diploma, he would have tried harder in school. And now that he was out looking for jobs, he saw there weren't very many things he was qualified to do. Vacuuming cars at the local car wash for minimum wage was the best he could come up with. At least he had stopped selling drugs. But when he saw me wearing a cap and gown in our school colors, he knew he had no one to blame but himself. I didn't know if *mi hermano* was going to turn the pain of this lesson into a positive force that would motivate him to get his act together, but I hoped so. After all, as Mrs. Javellano had said to me, it's never too late. But after taking a few photos, Rodrigo walked away to be alone with his thoughts and he was pretty quiet the rest of the day. Though he had been a real jerk to me for years, I still felt bad for him.

My younger brother Miguel, on the other hand, was bouncing around like a Mexican jumping bean. He particularly loved the tassel on my graduation hat.

"Take another picture," he told *mi papi* as he pulled off my graduation cap and put it on top of his nine-year-old head for like, the eleventh time in a row. "Take another picture of me and Sonia."

I leaned in and smiled once again as the flash went off. Seeing my younger brother goof around with my graduation cap filled my heart with joy. For the first time in his life, I—a girl—was his role model. And something told me that he too would one day wear a tassel of his own.

"*Geraldo, ven aquí,*" I said, quickly pulling him by the arm. "And bring the camera; I want you to meet someone."

I dragged Geraldo through the crowd and positioned myself right behind Tee-Ay so she would bump into me with her next step.

"Oops, excuse me," she said, colliding into me.

"Hello, Tee-Ay," I answered.

"Sonia," she said with a big smile on her face. We hugged. "So good to see you, girl. What is up?"

"Well," I told her, "I am starting community college in the fall."

"Amazing," she said with genuine happiness for me. Tee-Ay had never been one of those fake girls in high school who smiled all the time and told you nice things but then talked trash about you behind your back. She had always been a true friend.

"I mean, I know it's not USC, but—"

She cut me off. "Don't even think like that, Sonia. Really, that is awesome."

"But I won't be able to take a full load of classes 'cause I need to work at my cousin's auto shop as a bookkeeper for some money, but . . ." I continued. I knew that making the investment in going to college would be the best money I'd ever spent. In one of those home studies packets I had even seen a chart explaining how people with college diplomas usually made at least a million dollars more over the course of their life than people who didn't go to college. But still, it wasn't right that *mi papi* had to work so hard to support me now that I was out of high school. The cash I was earning, along with Rigo's small income, helped make it possible for *mi papi* to take an extra two nights a week off so that he could stay home, relax, and spend some time on the couch with his *familia*.

"Well, you know how it is," I said to Tee-Ay.

"Sonia," interrupted Geraldo, eager to get a good shot of me and Tee-Ay. "*Una* picture, *una sola*, come on."

"Geraldo, *ven*," I said, ignoring the camera and waving him closer. "I want you to meet one of my best friends in the whole world. This is Tee-Ay, the girl I told you about." I turned. "Tee-Ay, this is my boyfriend, Geraldo."

It was the first time I had used the word *boyfriend* to introduce Geraldo. Tee-Ay stared at him in a daze, like she had never seen such a hot guy in all her life. I knew how she felt, though. Geraldo was absolutely gorgeous and I had been starting to notice other chicks checking him out, even when I was standing right next to him. Girls were such bitches. Of course I got jealous, but once, when Geraldo saw me getting snippy, he pulled me aside and said, "Sonia, I only have *ojos* for you, *amor*. Remember . . . it's been written."

Then we kissed. It was magical. The tenderness in his lips was so gentle, and the trueness in his eyes was so pure, it became for me the moment in my life when I realized that someday Geraldo and I would be married. He was the love of my life, and I was the love of his. We were two people with one soul.

It really was like he had always said: *It has been written.*

Incredibly, the fairy tales were correct. *Príncipe* Charming does exist. And he's smoking-hot, too.

"Very nice to meet you," Geraldo said to Tee-Ay in his usual suave, gentlemanlike manner. He extended his hand in warm greeting.

"Hi," Tee-Ay said, trying to pretend she was all calm, cool, and collected.

"Congratulations on your good news," Geraldo said to her. "Sonia has told me many nice things about you. I hope that maybe one day we can all go out for a lunch. It will be my treat."

"I would love to have lunch sometime," Tee-Ay responded, then she looked at me with a twinkle in her eye. "But it will have to be french fries—"

"And a Diet Pepsi," I said, finishing her sentence. We both laughed.

"Well," Geraldo answered, not getting the inside joke about our old *tradición*, "it is a strange lunch, this one you talk about, but if that is what you wish, okay." Then he stepped back and lifted the camera. "Now, how about a picture?"

Tee-Ay and I pressed our cheeks together and smiled, and Geraldo took a picture that I still have today—it just came out so perfect. Tee-Ay and I hugged again.

"I am so proud of you," she told me.

"And what do you expect me to say about you?" I replied. "Lunch for sure?" I said.

"*Fo' sure!*" she answered. Our lifelong friendship had been rekindled, and we knew that we would be there for one another for the rest of our lives.

Sí, high school graduation had been a very proud day for me. But my schooling did not end there. Two years later I ended up graduating with an Associate of Arts degree from a two-year community college and was then accepted to a four-year university. When I got the news, I raced to the woman who had been there for me my whole life. Or at least my whole second life. She cried like I was her own daughter.

"You make my heart want to burst, *mija*," Mrs. Javellano said as she gave me a big hug. Though I had already graduated high school, we had made it a point to share *champurrados vainillas* as often as we could.

"I could not have done any of this without you," I replied, holding the college acceptance letter. "You were the one who showed me the way."

"Yes you could have, Sonia," she replied. "And you would have, too. What's that your *papi* calls you—*tortuguita*?"

She looked at me and smiled. There was deep warmth in her eyes. And then a hint of concern.

"*Mija*, are things better yet with your *ama*?" she asked.

I paused.

"No," I answered. "Not really."

Though *mi papi* and I remained as close as ever, my relationship with *mi ama* had never really healed. A part of me never forgave her for all the things she had done to me growing up, but another part of me didn't want to live the rest of my life being angry at her either. I guess the way she raised me had been the only way she knew how. I try to be polite to her nowadays when we see each other, but we're definitely not close. Looking back, I don't think we were ever close. That hurts me. However, I have a feeling it will help me later in life. Especially in my career. My theory is, just like you can't be a good cook unless you really like to eat, you can't be a good family therapist unless you come from a screwed-up family.

That's what I want to do, become a family therapist. And heck, when you consider all my whacked-out relatives, I might end up being the best family therapist that ever lived!

That's funny. But maybe I shouldn't say that. Really, I don't want to hurt anybody's feelings.

So, after two years at community college and with the support of Mrs. Javellano, *mi papi*, and Geraldo, I made a plan for what I was going to do: finish my bachelor's degree, get a master's degree, and become a licensed counselor.

I guess, ultimately, I just like to help people.

Plus, I'll make a solid living too. There would be a good salary, I'll invest in a 401K retirement plan, and I'll get covered by proper health insurance so I can go see real doctors instead of rude nurses at overcrowded public *clínicas*.

But most important, on the last Friday of every month I'll be able to give Maria a reason to wait in an incredibly long line. After all, there's a deaf little girl down in Mexico who's going to need all the support I can send.

I guess *es verdad* what my people say . . . *Familia es todo*.

Family is everything.